She turned to him as she unbuckled her seatbelt. "Thank you, Thomas, for a lovely evening. You are always looking out for me. You are truly my best friend."

His gaze held hers, steady and unreadable. "Who wants to be more."

Kendrea inhaled sharply, her fingers stilling against the strap of her bag.

"I have always wanted to be more," Thomas continued, his voice quieter but no less firm. "You know it. And I'm tired of being just your friend."

Kendrea closed her eyes, drawing in a shaky breath. When she opened them, Thomas had moved closer.

And then he kissed her.

His lips were warm and firm against hers, catching her completely off guard. For a moment, she froze, her mind racing to make sense of what was happening.

But then—almost as if some deep, hidden part of her finally broke free—she found herself responding. Her hands instinctively reached up to rest on his chest, feeling the rapid beat of his heart beneath her palms. The kiss was slow, deliberate, filled with a mixture of longing and certainty that left no room for doubt.

When they finally broke apart, both of them were breathing heavily, the air between them charged with an electricity she couldn't ignore.

"Thomas," Kendrea whispered, her voice trembling. "What are we doing?"

THROUGH THICK AND THIN

BRENDA BARRETT

THROUGH THICK AND THIN

A Jamaica Treasures Book/February 2025
Published by Jamaica Treasures
Manchester, Jamaica

This is a work of fiction. Names, characters, places, and incidents are either the product of the author's imagination or are used fictitiously. Any resemblance to an actual person or persons, living or dead, events, or locales is entirely coincidental.

ISBN 978-976-97430-3-8

ALSO BY BRENDA BARRETT

FULL CIRCLE
NEW BEGINNINGS
THE PREACHER AND THE PROSTITUTE
AFTER THE END
THE EMPTY HAMMOCK
THE PULL OF FREEDOM
REBOUND SERIES
THREE RIVERS SERIES
NEW SONG SERIES
BANCROFT SERIES
MAGNOLIA SISTERS SERIES
SCARLETT SERIES
WILEY BROTHERS SERIES
PRYCE SISTERS SERIES
THE JACKSONS SERIES
CRIMSON HILL SERIES
SPICE AND STONE SERIES
RIDGEVIEW SERIES

ABOUT THE AUTHOR

Brenda Barrett is an award-winning and bestselling author who has a passion for writing real Jamaican romances.

When she's not weaving words that transport readers to exotic locales, you can find her nurturing her green thumb in the garden or doting on her beloved cats.

With an infectious zest for life, this author brings a unique perspective to her writing that is both relatable and thought-provoking.

Don't be surprised if you find yourself lost in the pages of her latest work, as she seamlessly blends romance with some drama, mystery, and suspense, or even sci-fi, leaving readers wanting more.

You can connect with Brenda online at:
Brenalbar.com
Twitter.com/AuthorWriterBB
Facebook.com/AuthorBrendaBarrett

Chapter One

Kendrea eagerly walked into the semi-dark interior of Howie's Pub. She was meeting her friend Tiffany to discuss catering for her sister Kenny's wedding. Afterward, she was having dinner with Thomas. He had told her to meet him here—he had something important to ask her. They had been hanging out more often than usual these days, and quite inexplicably, she was growing more and more attracted to him.

It was baffling. He was the same old Thomas—her chubby friend from high school who could make her laugh through tears, her favorite pal. What had changed? Why was she suddenly seeing him in a different light this past year?

It was that date to the Chamber of Commerce dinner. Thomas had kissed her when he dropped her home. She had laughed it off, but that kiss had kept her up that night. She had never been kissed like that before. She still got tremors in her lower body just thinking about it.

Suddenly, Thomas Sterling—her overweight friend, who was also her stepbrother since their parents had gotten married five years ago—was now the star of all her fantasies.

She was completely thrown by her feelings. Kendrea had always valued their friendship—solid, unshakable, built on years of trust and shared memories. But now, every time Thomas was near, her pulse raced, and she couldn't ignore how her gaze lingered on him a little longer than it should. His laugh, once a comforting sound, now lit something deep within her.

She glanced around the pub, spotting Tiffany already seated at a booth and scrolling through her phone. Kendrea waved and made her way over, brushing off the nervous energy buzzing under her skin. She needed to focus. Wedding catering came first, not the growing mess of emotions swirling around Thomas.

"Kenny better appreciate this," Tiffany said with a grin as Kendrea slid into the booth. "I've called in favors from my best vendors."

"You're the best," Kendrea said, flashing her a smile, but her mind was already drifting to Thomas. What did he wanted to discuss?

"Earth to Kendrea?" Tiffany's voice broke through her thoughts. "You okay? You look a little... distracted."

"Oh, sorry," Kendrea said quickly, shaking her head. "Just a long day. Since I did Jairo and Audra's place, I've been getting offers left, right, and center. I'll have to expand the business soon."

"That's a great problem to have," Tiffany said. "I have the same problem too. After I catered their wedding, I've had quite a few bookings, and it's all thanks to you."

"Don't mention it," Kendrea said. "We look out for each other. So, let's talk wedding."

"Okay," Tiffany nodded. They chit-chatted for a while as Kendrea took notes to double-check with her sister and Camden.

"So, who will you be bringing as your plus-one?" Tiffany asked as they finished up their pressing business.

"No one," Kendrea said, waving her off. "I haven't been in a relationship for close to a year."

Tiffany smiled. "And besides, Thomas will be there. What on earth do you see in the guy? Apart from his personality, I mean. He's huge. He looks like a supersized Pillsbury Doughboy with curly, unruly hair. And can't you get him to shave? Good Lord, the beard adds another twenty pounds to him."

Kendrea stiffened at Tiffany's words, her smile fading. A surge of defensiveness rose in her chest, but she forced herself to keep her tone light. "Well, thankfully, I'm not shallow enough to judge someone by their size or beard length."

Tiffany's brows shot up. "Whoa, relax! I didn't mean to hit a nerve. I just... I guess I don't get it. You're drop-dead gorgeous, K. You could have any guy you want."

Kendrea offered a tight smile, the heat of annoyance simmering just below the surface. "Thomas is amazing, Tiff. He's kind, funny, dependable—more than I can say for most guys I've met."

Tiffany raised her hands in surrender. "Okay, okay, I get it. No judgment here. If he makes you happy, that's what matters." She paused, then added with a teasing grin, "But are you sure there's nothing going on? You're awfully quick to defend him."

Kendrea felt her cheeks warm, but she shook her head. "There's nothing going on. We're just... close."

"Uh-huh," Tiffany said, clearly unconvinced. "Well, if

you ever want to talk about it, you know where to find me."

Before Kendrea could respond Thomas walked into the pub and looked around. He was in a good mood, his rotund figure practically bristling with it.

He was wearing his signature blue jeans and a navy shirt that looked as if it were about to burst around his belly. He had actually shaved his beard—thank goodness, it had not been doing him any favors.

He still had his hair long, though at least he had brushed it back and tied it in a ponytail. He was clearly a good-looking guy, even with the extra weight. If you squinted hard enough, you could see similarities to Will Demps, the half-Korean, half-Black NFL player turned model. They had similar facial features, in her biased opinion. Thomas had the same genetic makeup—his mother was Korean, and his father was Black Jamaican.

He had the same strong jawline, a bit of a cleft chin, and those dark, almond-shaped eyes that could melt you if you weren't careful. His features weren't as sharp—far from it—but the resemblance was enough that Kendrea had often caught herself daydreaming about the comparison. Of course, she would never admit that aloud.

He caught sight of her and waved, his face lighting up with that trademark grin—the one that always made her heart skip just a little. It was a warm, genuine smile as if he was glad to see her, even when they were hanging out casually.

She stood up, smoothing her hands over her jeans. "I'll see you later, Tiff. Thanks again for helping with the wedding."

"Sure thing," Tiffany said, eyeing her with a knowing smirk. "Have fun with Pillsbury."

Kendrea rolled her eyes but didn't respond. She met Thomas halfway across the pub, her pulse quickening as he smiled down at her.

"Hey, Kendrea," he said, his deep voice sending a shiver down her spine. "Hope I'm not interrupting. I assumed you guys would be done by now."

"We are done," she replied, her voice softer than she intended. "Ready for dinner?"

"Yeah, but, uh..." He hesitated, rubbing the back of his neck. "Can we talk first? There's something I've been meaning to ask you."

Kendrea's stomach flipped. "Sure," she said, gesturing to an empty table nearby. "What's on your mind?"

As they sat down, Thomas leaned forward, his expression uncharacteristically serious. "Kendrea, I've been meaning to tell you this. I can't keep it in any longer. I met someone. It's getting serious."

"What?" Kendrea frowned. "When? Who?"

Thomas chuckled. "Remember Amanda from high school?"

Kendrea's heart dropped into her stomach, and she forced herself to sit still, not letting her shock show. "Of course, I remember her. She was one of the girls who wouldn't give you the time of day. She teased you with her friends."

"But now she likes me. Like, really, really likes me," Thomas said, a hint of disbelief still in his voice. "She lives in the States, came out for my buddy Griffin's wedding, and we started chatting. Before you know it, we made a connection."

Kendrea blinked, her mind racing. She wanted to ask him a million questions. What did she do? Was she using him like so many others? As big as he was, that did not deter the girls from flocking to Thomas. He was wealthy, he drove a nice vehicle, and he was a sensitive soul. He usually fell for their sob stories until he found out they were using him.

Then he would get depressed and complain to her about nobody loving him for who he was.

"I hope Amanda is not going to trample on your self-esteem like the others," Kendrea said.

"I doubt that," Thomas said. "Amanda is a health and fitness coach."

"She is?" Kendrea raised an eyebrow.

"Yup. Certified, degreed, and runs her own business. She offered to move out here and be my coach for six months. She has a chef partner who will do all my meals."

"And you will pay her?" Kendrea asked skeptically.

"Yes. She's doing a service," Thomas said, getting annoyed.

"How much?" Kendrea asked suspiciously.

"Enough," Thomas said shiftily. "And that's what I want to talk to you about."

"What?" Kendrea asked.

"I want her to stay at my Ridgeview house. I'm going to be there too."

"And you want me to decorate it for you and your new lady love," Kendrea sighed, "and your chef?"

"She's not my new lady love," Thomas said quickly. "We had a connection—that's all I said. You raced to conclusions. But you sound jealous, and I like that." He looked smug.

"I am not jealous," Kendrea snorted. "I am just completely flabbergasted by how gullible you are with these women. Last year, it was Nicole. Remember her? She sent a recording to Abby—your cousin—saying she was sleeping with you because she wanted to milk you for all you had. This year, it's Amanda. Next year, it will be someone else."

Thomas sighed. "I'm twenty-six years old, an overweight guy with all the needs and desires of any normal male. The one woman I want, above anyone else, has shoved me into the friend zone. What do you suggest I do, Kendrea? Live like a monk? Slink around the place and beg for scraps of affection? No, thanks. I'm tired of waiting around for something that's never going to happen."

Kendrea's heart skipped at his words, and for a moment, she didn't know how to respond. She'd always been there for Thomas—listening to him complain about his love life and encouraging him when he was down, but hearing him talk like this felt different. It stung.

"I didn't put you in the friend zone, Thomas," she scoffed at the idea. "We've always been friends. You were the one who decided to change the status quo a couple of months ago when you kissed me after the Chamber of Commerce dinner. Until then, I didn't even know you liked me like that. You were always chasing after one girl or another and telling me about them."

"To make you jealous!" Thomas said. "And you never got the message!"

"I got the message when you kissed me," Kendrea said. "Admittedly, I liked it. I can't stop thinking about it. I was contemplating taking things further. I even thought this was what this wretched dinner was about. I thought we were finally going to clear the air, but instead, you're telling me that you've met someone with whom you have a connection—again. I feel like a clown."

"Wait, hold up," Thomas said. "You're saying if there was no Amanda, you would seriously date me?"

"Yes! Maybe! I don't know," Kendrea growled. "I shouldn't even be telling you anything now that you have Amanda."

Thomas looked at her in shock. "Well, this adds a new spin to things. I was going to ask you to move in with us at Ridgeview and act as a buffer. I don't want to be blindsided again by someone out to use me. I thought you would be perfect to sniff things out. After all, you clocked Nicole from the very beginning, and you can read people's intentions like a book. But in light of these new revelations, maybe you don't want to help."

"I wouldn't say that," Kendrea said. "I've been dying to decorate one of those Ridgeview houses to my taste and I know you'll let me do whatever I want, so that's a plus."

Thomas nodded. "Please don't ask me anything about colors and whatnot. And you'll have to consult with Amanda about the gym. I told her I have a blank slate. She was excited about that."

"I'm going to put Amanda and her chef in the guest house," Kendrea said. "Is the chef male or female?"

"Female," Thomas replied. "They're a two-for-one deal. Amanda says she'll prepare delicious, nutritious meals."

"Okay, I'll do it. I'll move in for six months. When does Amanda want to start?"

"As soon as possible," Thomas said.

He looked at her with curiosity. "So, when you said you were thinking about us, what were you thinking exactly?"

"Nothing," Kendrea muttered. "Forget it."

Chapter Two

But he couldn't forget it, Thomas thought darkly while driving home. Maybe he had overplayed the emphasis on having a connection with Amanda. Maybe he had said one too many reallys when he said she liked him. But Kendrea had not reacted as he had expected, which was bothering him greatly.

All of this was just an elaborate plan to make Kendrea come and live with him. If she became jealous of Amanda in the process and realized that she could be more than friends with him, that would make him happy.

This was all his best friend Griffin's idea. After hearing him worry himself to death about the kiss after the Chamber of Commerce dinner and how Kendrea had shrugged it off, Griffin told him to give him a chance to strategize the situation and devise a solution.

He thought his childhood friend just wanted him to shut up. He had gone a bit overboard with his whining and complaining about Kendrea just seeing him as a friend, but Griffin really had a plan—he wasn't the chief marketing strategist at CSO Solutions, one of the leading marketing companies in the Caribbean and Latin America, for nothing.

"I have a plan for you," Griffin had said in the dressing room when they were getting ready at the hotel for his wedding. His friend was marrying his childhood sweetheart, Tracy, and he should have been focusing on his big day.

"Shouldn't you be focusing on your big day?" Thomas had frowned.

"I am," Griffin said, shrugging on his vest, "but I can do two things at once, can't I?"

Thomas nodded. "I guess."

"So I invited Amanda Pierce today."

"Amanda Pierce... the name seems familiar."

"That's because she is familiar. You were in the same class with her when they held you back because of your dysgraphia."

"Ah, yes. She and her little posse used to bully me. They called me Dumbfat. I hated that nickname. Out of all the stupid ones they called me, I detested that one the most. People were all over the place saying, 'Hey, Dumbfat.'"

"I know," Griffin said. "I remember. They called me Dumfat's best friend Dumbslim."

"And to add insult to injury," Thomas said, "Amanda told the whole school that I had a crush on her and was following her around like a dog."

"Nobody believed that," Griffin snorted. "You had Kendrea Carter as a friend—the prettiest girl in the school."

"Then why on earth did you invite Amanda to your wedding?" Thomas frowned.

"Because she could be the answer to a couple of your problems."

"I'm listening." Thomas looked at his friend with anticipation. He didn't quite know where he was going with this.

"She's a health and fitness coach. She helped Tracy lose weight for the wedding."

"I did notice that Tracy is looking much slimmer," Thomas said. "I never thought to ask how she did it."

"She used Amanda and her sister, Stephanie, to help. They got her on an exercise routine, fixed all her meals, moved into her apartment for six weeks, and turned it around for her.

"Oh really," Thomas raised an eyebrow.

"I was skeptical at first because they were expensive, but Tracy didn't mind paying for their service. It paid off in the end."

Thomas nodded.

"Amanda and Steph are trying to establish themselves in the local market. Amanda earned her degree in nutrition and exercise and worked for two years at a wellness center that treats obesity. Stephanie is a wellness chef who used to work at a wellness resort in Florida. Amanda's work permit expired, and there were issues with the renewal, so her sister Steph came out to help her start her business. For now, they're looking at private clients until they can establish themselves."

"Interesting," Thomas said. "So how does any of that affect me?"

"You want to lose weight. You just bought a posh house. You want to make Kendrea realize she loves you, so I put all those facts together and came up with a solution."

"What's the solution?" Thomas frowned. He honestly couldn't see what any of these things had to do with each other.

"Move in Amanda as your fitness coach, Stephanie as your chef, and tell Kendrea you're in love with Amanda. Ask her to act as a chaperone."

"Nope. No." Thomas shook his head.

"Think about it," Griffin urged. "It's a foolproof plan. You'll lose weight and get the girl of your dreams in the process."

"How would that work, though?" Thomas asked.

"Just make Kendrea jealous!" Griffin said, "You said it yourself that you observed that Kendrea gets extra affectionate when she thinks you are interested in someone else."

"Mmmph," Thomas muttered, "I'll think about it."

"Don't think about it too long." Griffin stood back from the mirror. "How do I look?"

"Like you just stepped off the cover of GQ magazine," Thomas said, looking at his friend proudly. Griffin was a handsome fellow, slim and athletically built. He had always envied his friend's natural leanness. Griffin could eat piles of food without gaining a pound. In fact, Griffin could out-eat him any day.

"We'll discuss the plan some more when I return from my honeymoon," Griffin said. "It's a great plan, you'll see."

Thomas didn't know about that. The moment he had seen Amanda at the reception, he had vividly remembered the many ways she had teased him in high school. One never really forgot their bullies. She was still pretty and carried herself with confidence, and he had smiled faintly in her direction, raising his glass at her in what he had thought would be a mock salute.

But she had made a beeline over to him and smiled genuinely, "Thomas Sterling, how are you?"

"Good. Great," he had smiled back.

"I am so sorry for how I treated you in high school," she said without preamble, "I have always wanted to say I am sorry."

"Is that so?" He raised an eyebrow.

Amanda nodded. "I am very sorry. I have turned over a new leaf since then. I work in the health sciences now, and I have seen firsthand how bullying can cause low self-esteem and other lasting issues. I've always regretted the part I played in making high school difficult for you."

Thomas was taken aback. He had expected snark or avoidance, not an outright apology. He remembered shifting uncomfortably, unsure whether to forgive her or brush it off. Griffin's plan was in his head, though.

"Water under the bridge," he had said after a pause, keeping his tone light. "We were all young and stupid once."

Amanda smiled, a little flirtatiously. "I hope you don't mind taking my business card. Griffin told me you were looking for someone with a strong background in fitness and nutrition to turn things around for you. I'd love the opportunity to work with you."

Thomas took the card, glancing at it briefly before tucking it into his pocket. "I'll think about it," he said noncommittally.

He had thought about it for weeks after the wedding until, finally, he had capitulated. He would hire Amanda for six months. The truth was, he wanted to lose weight and be with Kendrea. If his theory was true—that she was in denial about him—then he was right to execute Griffin's plan.

So far, Kendrea's reaction was what he had hoped for and more. She had seemed quite jealous at the thought of Amanda being with him. She had even admitted that she was thinking about him romantically. He had to play this delicately. He didn't want Kendrea to believe he was some kind of player.

The thought of him as a player had him quietly chuckling to himself. As much as he was outgoing and gregarious around people, including women, deep down, he was the insecure boy they used to call Dumbfat.

He turned up the car radio when he heard Brian McKnight's Back at One. He had it in his head that this was his and Kendrea's song. Well, his song for her.

He had always wanted her and believed there was something between them, but she had never let herself see it. Maybe she never would. But if there was even a chance, even the smallest sliver of hope, he was willing to take it.

The song swelled in his ears, the lyrics echoing his own silent resolve: One, you're like a dream come true; two, just wanna be with you; Three, girl, it's plain to see that you're the only one for me...

This time, he wouldn't just wait for Kendrea to figure things out. This time, he was going to make sure she saw him—the real him. No more waiting for the right moment, no more playing it safe. He was going to be bold. This time, he was going to show her that they were meant to be.

Chapter Three

Kendrea had too many things on her plate. Squeezing in Amanda for a meeting with her tight schedule was an additional burden she could do without, but the lady had insisted. And now, here they were, staring at each other like combatants across Kendrea's desk.

To make matters worse, Amanda looked shockingly good. She had been a pretty girl in high school, but now she was practically glowing with health. If she had on makeup, it was superbly done. Her bronze complexion was flawless, her body was leanly muscular, and her natural curls were long and juicy-looking. Kendrea almost caught herself from touching her recently straightened hair; she had wanted a change from her curls, but now she had curl envy.

Amanda smiled at her. "Kendrea, you haven't changed a bit since I last saw you. How are you doing?"

"Fine," Kendrea said abruptly. She didn't return the pleasantries. Amanda was probably fishing for compliments, hoping that Kendrea would say, "Well, you have changed, you look fit and fabulous." She would rather bite her tongue than say that out loud. Amanda had been a bully in high school, and it would take much more than a compliment for her to forget that.

"I have ten minutes," Kendrea said briskly. "I have a meeting across town with a prospective client, and there is traffic."

Amanda nodded. "I understand. I have a meeting after this, too, with Thomas. This should not take long. I was told you were the person responsible for decorating his place in Ridgeview."

Kendrea nodded. She had started furnishing the house a week ago. It was the most fun project she had ever done. Money wasn't an object, and she could walk into the furniture warehouse and live out her fantasies, ordering all the furniture she would if she were doing her own space.

"Well, you haven't called me to consult on the gym space," Amanda said. "What gives?"

"I haven't gotten around to that yet," Kendrea said. "I have it on my checklist for next week."

"Well, could you move it up?" Amanda asked. "My time with Thomas starts in three weeks. I want to ensure that everything is in place before I begin. Exercise, more specifically weight training, is a vital part of my program."

"Tell me about your program," Kendrea narrowed her eyes suspiciously. "And why did you set your sights on Thomas? I can clearly remember you and your friends teasing him in high school."

"We were idiots," Amanda said. "We thought it was funny at the time, but honestly, it wasn't. Thomas didn't deserve that." Amanda's expression softened, a flicker of remorse crossing her face. "I've apologized to him since then, and I'm trying to make amends in my own way. My program helps people not just with their bodies but with their confidence too. Thomas could use some of that."

Kendrea raised an eyebrow. "And you think you're the person to give it to him?"

"I do," Amanda said, her tone firm. "I've been doing this for a while now. Weight training, nutrition, mindset coaching—it's all part of the package. Thomas has potential, but he needs a push, someone to believe in him and help him see it through. And no offense to you, I know you two are close, but this is not your area of expertise. It's mine. I've coached hundreds, if not thousands, of clients, and they have not only lost weight but kept it off."

"Thousands?" Kendrea raised an eyebrow. "We graduated high school seven years ago. Since then, I assume you went to college like I did, did an internship with someone more qualified in your field for at least a year, and then ventured out independently. That would be a generous two years."

Amanda widened her eyes. "Well, er... you are mostly accurate. I shouldn't have said thousands; I misspoke."

"You mean I caught you in a lie?" Kendrea leaned forward. "Have you even helped ten people lose weight? Do you have any references?"

"I already gave Thomas those details; he is my client," Amanda said waspishly. "If you want to know more, maybe you should become a client."

"If I lose any more weight, I'd be emaciated," Kendrea snuffed. "But say I did take you up on your offer, how much does it cost? Let's say I am commissioning you to stay at my place for six months while you do your thing—whatever it is that you claim you do."

Amanda glared at her. "That is not a serious inquiry. You want to know how much Thomas is paying me."

"I do want to know," Kendrea said. "If you don't tell me, I'll stall you. I'll have so many excuses for not completing the décor at the house your head would spin, and Thomas would just accept them."

Amanda sighed. "My base charge for a guy of Thomas' size is ten thousand US per month."

Kendrea widened her eyes. "My goodness. I am torn between asking you how I can get your gig and being outraged that you are charging Thomas so much money while you are staying at his place for free. This is the grift to end all grifts."

"I am cheaper in the long run than treating an obesity-related disease such as diabetes or heart failure," Amanda snapped, crossing her arms defensively. "And I'm not grifting. I'm providing a service that changes lives. Thomas understands that and values it enough to make the investment."

Kendrea smirked, leaning forward. "Relax, Amanda. I'm not saying you're not worth it. But ten grand a month? That's serious money. I just hope Thomas knows exactly what he's signing up for."

Amanda exhaled, her tone softening slightly. "He does. I've been very transparent with him. And for the record, I'm not freeloading at his house. I offered to find my own accommodation, but Thomas insisted. He said it would be more efficient for me to stay there and monitor his progress closely."

"How convenient," Kendrea murmured, not bothering to hide the sarcasm.

Amanda's eyes narrowed. "You know, Kendrea, I get that you're protective of Thomas. That's great. But I'm here to help him, not take advantage of him. If you can't see that, maybe you're the one with the problem."

Kendrea tilted her head, her smirk fading. "I just want to

ensure he's not being played, that's all."

"And he's not," Amanda said firmly. "I don't have to tell you this, but to get some breathing room from you, I will give you an example of my most recent client. Her name is Paula Tinsdale. She was diagnosed with type 2 diabetes and was overweight. My chef, Stephanie, and I turned her around. Paula not only lost weight, but we reversed her diabetes and cured it. Her doctors were amazed."

"Oh, wow," Kendrea widened her eyes. "That's amazing, if true. Don't believe I won't be checking to see if it's true. Isn't Paula Tinsdale, Richard Tinsdale's aunt? I know her. I haven't seen her for a while, but I remember when she was huge."

"Check away," Amanda said. "Paula sings our praises wherever we go. That's how we met Tracy, whom I'm sure you know. We helped her lose twenty pounds in six weeks for her wedding." Amanda paused. "Now, about the gym, I have the specs right here. I need these exact pieces of equipment."

She handed Kendrea a piece of paper with an equipment list, another with pictures of the equipment, and a final one with the total layout. Amanda was professional; it would make her life easier.

Kendrea thought resentfully that she had been quite prepared to dislike Amanda. And maybe she still did. Thomas liked her, and that was usually enough for her to automatically dislike any female on his radar.

She watched Amanda leave and then stared into space, wondering what the difference was between being protective of someone and jealous of them.

The truth was, she didn't know if there was a difference when it came to Thomas. As much as she liked to deny it, her feelings for him, even when they were children, had never been that clear-cut.

She remembered seeing him on that first day of school, feeling inexplicably drawn to him. She didn't know why. He had fascinated her. Everybody else had a different reaction. He was older, and the rumor was that they had kept him back in third form because the teachers couldn't understand his handwriting, so he couldn't pass any tests. He usually scored high on anything that didn't require writing—multiple choice tests, mathematics, physics—but he bombed at writing. Kendrea had felt for him. All his friends were in fifth form, talking about the external exams while he was stuck.

Nobody talked to him, so he mostly kept to himself. Then, in the second week of the new semester, his mother died. The rumor mill was rife again. His mother, Lin Sun Sterling, had gone to the dentist for a routine procedure and was allergic to the anesthesia. She had gone into anaphylactic shock and died before they could revive her.

Kendra didn't know what to say to him, but she remembered standing outside the classroom when she heard the news. Her heart squeezed painfully. She had lost her father while young as well. She knew that particular kind of hurt.

The other students whispered about it—some out of genuine shock, others out of curiosity. Some even made cruel jokes.

And then, that same day, she saw Amanda Pierce and her friends blocking Thomas in the hallway.

"Hey, Dumbfat?" Amanda had taunted. "Did you know even my two-year-old cousin can write?"

Kendrea hadn't thought twice. She walked right up and shoved Amanda aside.

"Leave him alone," she had snapped.

Amanda had rolled her eyes but backed off, muttering

something under her breath.

Thomas had just looked at her, his brown eyes dark with an emotion she couldn't quite place.

"They're just idiots," she had said awkwardly, shifting her weight. "Ignore them."

And that was how their friendship had begun.

She hadn't needed him to say thank you. He had just started sitting beside her in class and, eventually, talking to her. It had been easy, natural. They understood each other without needing to explain much.

That's how it had always been with them. Until June, the Chamber of Commerce Dinner, and the kiss.

She got up and started to pack up to leave. Her client was waiting, and if she started thinking about the kiss, she'd be late for the meeting.

Chapter Four

Kendrea was stuck in traffic in midtown Montego Bay when her prospective client asked her to reschedule for two hours later. She wasn't mad about it since her afternoon was wide open. In the interim, she could use the time to finalize the guest list for Kenny and Camden's engagement party. Instead of a bachelor or bachelorette party, the couple requested a joint party with their friends and family.

Kendrea was the point person for the party, but since it had grown into a massive pre-Christmas bash, she'd asked for help from both families and delegated tasks to ease the pressure. So far, it has been working well.

The party would be held in Camden's parents' backyard and their stepsister, Lori, would cater. Kenny had settled on a burgundy and silver theme, and Kendrea would handle the invitations and decorate the tables. Lorraine Byfield, Camden's mother, had everything else handled—she had thrown countless parties in the spacious backyard.

Kendrea would stop at Sterling Plaza, just three minutes away, grab something to eat at the restaurant, and chat with her stepsister Lori about the party and the latest developments in Thomas' love life.

Lori was almost as protective of Thomas as Kendrea was. Her ire would rise when Kendrea told her about Amanda—how Amanda had bullied Thomas in high school and made his life hell. And now, Amanda was back in his life as his health and fitness coach and potential love interest. It made zero sense to Kendrea why Thomas was entertaining Amanda, and she knew it wouldn't make any sense to Lori either.

Lori loved her brother without reservation, but she despaired about how vulnerable he was with women who saw him only as their meal ticket.

Their mother, Lin Sun Sterling, had passed away unexpectedly when they were young teenagers. The four children—Lori, Thomas, Chad, and Yasmin—had mourned her deeply. By all accounts, she had been a wonderful mother, and though they still had their father and grandparents at the time, Lori, being the oldest by eight years, had helped keep her younger siblings from falling apart.

Lori had been the mother hen of the Sterling siblings, and she was still at it, even though they were all grown. When Kendrea's mother, Grace Carter, married their father, George Sterling, five years ago, it had become a running joke that they had to ask permission from Lori.

Kendrea turned into the plaza, searching for a parking spot. The place was packed as usual. On the right side of the plaza was Deals on Wheels, Thomas' business. The three-story building housed the shop on the first floor, offices on the second, and four two-bedroom apartments on the third floor, where Thomas and his siblings lived. They'd refurbished the living space six years ago so everyone could have their own area. It was also around that time, when Thomas who was twenty, that his grandfather passed and left the business to him. Bless his old-fashioned heart, the old man had given everything to the oldest male.

Thomas had since rectified the inequity by acquiring the surrounding land and giving each of his siblings a building of their own to own and control. Lori's building housed her restaurant, Korean Fusion and a supermarket. Chad's building held tech-based shops, and he even rented to a mobile network. Yasmin's building, the newest on the block, would feature a lighting store, a furniture store, and Yasmin's architectural office. Kendrea's interior design business would fit right in. She'd already told Yasmin to reserve a space for her when the building was finished.

In her present location, Kendrea was tucked between a farm and a pet store, and she wanted out. Neither of these businesses complemented her own, and she was acutely aware that her office's exterior didn't reflect the aesthetic she wanted her brand to have. But Yasmin's building would be just right.

Her stomach rumbled loudly, and just then, someone backed out of a parking spot almost directly in front of Lori's Korean Fusion Restaurant.

Lori usually did brisk business. She served large portions, and the food was always tasty. The menu was varied, but Kendrea always stuck to her standard order—Korean fried chicken, bulgogi, and kimchi fried rice. She was boring like that, and the staff knew her order by heart.

Kendrea backed into the spot and looked across at Deals on Wheels. Though Thomas had a manager running the business, he usually stayed upstairs in his office, where he played the local and overseas stock markets.

"The best game in the world," he often declared. He had wanted to teach her how to trade, but they could never find a convenient time. Maybe now that they would be living in the same house, they'd have more time to work at it.

She stepped out of her car and took a deep breath. The warm scent of grilled meat and spices from Lori's restaurant made her mouth water. She glanced once more at Deals on Wheels. The business sold vehicles and auto parts and even offered servicing. The showroom now proudly displayed a sign: On Sale: Fully Electric Vehicles!

She smiled. It had been impressive to watch Thomas expand the family business. When his grandfather was in charge, Sterling Plaza had been a fraction of what it was now.

The plaza was bustling with customers coming and going, kids chasing each other in the open courtyard, and the sound of hammering coming from the new wing under construction.

Kendrea pushed open the door to the restaurant and was greeted by a calm, relaxing décor. She had convinced Lori to ease up on the red and black tones that had previously made the space feel cramped and too aggressive—like walking into a high-stakes poker den instead of a cozy eatery. Surprisingly, Lori had agreed to let Kendrea redecorate to space. The place felt welcoming and inviting, with muted earth tones, soft lighting, and warm wooden tables.

There was a line at the cashier, and people were waiting for their orders, but Kendrea wasn't about to go through that. She knew Lori was probably in the back.

She called her while heading toward a cozy corner table by the window. The spot gave her a perfect view of the plaza, including the new wing that she hoped would soon house her business.

"Hey, Lady," Lori answered.

"I'm here, sitting by the window," Kendrea said. "The line is long. Can I get the VIP treatment, please?"

"But of course," Lori chuckled. "Am I to assume your order remains the same as it always is?"

"You would assume right," Kendrea laughed.

"I'll join you in a bit," Lori said, hanging up.

Kendrea checked her email while she waited. Kenny had sent her the guest list for the party, including their email addresses. She scanned it and then gasped. Nicole Pink was on the list—Thomas' ex. She was Alan's plus one. No way. No how. That was not happening, not under her watch.

She immediately fired off an email to Kenny:

I see you have Nicole Pink on your guest list. Please tell Camden that Nicole is not allowed at family events. She is Thomas' ex, remember?

"Oh, my bad, I didn't check Camden's side of the list thoroughly. I am snowed under with work," Kenny texted back. "Could you tell Camden, please? I may forget and then cause problems. I don't want problems at the party."

Kendrea called Camden immediately.

Camden answered. "Hey, sister-in-law, what's up?"

"I'm looking at the invitation list, and I see Alan Byfield is taking Nicole Pink as his plus one. That can't happen—she is Thomas' ex. They did not part on good terms."

"Oh," Camden murmured. "I'll rectify it immediately. Is that all?"

"For now," Kendrea said, "I am still combing through the list."

Camden chuckled. "You sound militant."

"I hated what she did to Thomas," Kendrea said. "I saw her name and saw red."

"I understand," Camden said. "Consider it handled."

She continued looking through the list, still fuming about Nicole. Of course, she had moved on, and it had to be with an upwardly mobile rich guy. She hoped Alan Byfield knew what he was getting into.

Nicole Pink chose her boyfriends with calculating efficiency. A year and a half ago, she was with Thomas so that he could finance her business, a clothing store named Pink'd. Kendrea had not trusted her one bit, and she had said as much to Thomas, who had shrugged off her misgivings.

Kendrea gritted her teeth. Every time she saw Nicole's name, it was enough to get her upset. She made a face and scrolled through the nearly two hundred names.

She would not go through any of this when she was getting married. She would do it small and intimate, like Audra and Jairo's backyard wedding. She would only have immediate family and close friends, a reception filled with people who genuinely wished her well. Kenny and Camden had allowed both sets of parents to hijack their simple wedding plans. Camden's parents were the ones footing the bill for the engagement party, and the guest list had exploded to the point that it now included Nicole Pink.

"You are frowning," Lori said, sliding into the seat across from her and untying her apron. "I didn't know you were dropping by today."

"Client pushed back our meeting time," Kendrea replied, setting her phone down and smiling at her stepsister. Lori had recently cut her wavy hair into a chin-length bob and dyed it a fiery shade of red. She had dramatically drawn cat-eye makeup emphasizing her almond-shaped eyes and high cheekbones. She looked striking, as always, with a confidence that radiated through her every movement.

"I love the new look," Kendrea said, gesturing to Lori's hair. "It suits you."

"Thanks," Lori replied, brushing a strand of hair behind her ear. "Figured it was time for a change. Life's too short to be boring."

Kendrea laughed softly. "You've got a point. Speaking of changes, I'm going to be moving in with Thomas at his new Ridgeview house."

Lori grinned. "Okay. Finally. Woohoo!"

"It's not like that," Kendrea chuckled. "Though it's good to know you will be supportive if Thomas and I get serious."

"A hundred percent," Lori nodded. "But if you are not moving in together, what's the situation?"

"He wants me there as a chaperone to his new health and fitness coach, Amanda, and she will bring her chef, Stephanie."

"What in the harem is going on?" Lori frowned.

Kendrea chuckled. "Thomas is finally doing something about his weight."

"And it takes three women to help him do it?" Lori frowned.

Kendrea laughed. "Apparently, he connected with Amanda at Griffin's wedding, and she suggested she could be his health and fitness coach. My one problem with her is that she used to bully him in high school. She and her little crew would tease him to tears."

"What?" Lori widened her eyes.

"Yup," Kendrea nodded. "They were brutal. And now he likes her and is paying her big money to help him shed the pounds."

"Goodness," Lori whistled. "On one hand, I'm happy he's doing something about the weight; that's how grandpa died—complications from obesity. I've been urging Thomas to get his weight under control, but he emotionally eats, and gets bigger after every breakup. But on the other hand, I am alarmed that this may not be serious. What do you know about Amanda, besides her mean girl reputation in high school?"

"Nothing much," Kendrea said. "I met with her earlier. She seems professional, but, as you know, looks can be deceiving. She said she cured Paula Tinsdale of diabetes. I will be investigating those claims."

"Thank you," Lori said. "I would join you in checking this woman out, but this month is crazy, and I am catering for the engagement party in two weeks. Are there any changes to the plans?"

"None," Kendrea said. "Everything is as it should be. The guest list is still two hundred, and the menu selections are the same."

Their conversation was interrupted as the server arrived with Kendrea's order. The familiar aroma of crispy Korean fried chicken, savory bulgogi, and spicy kimchi fried rice made her stomach growl in anticipation. She picked up her fork and took her first bite, savoring the explosion of flavors.

"So," Lori said, leaning in with a knowing look. "When you live with Thomas, maybe you two can get a romance going. You two would make such beautiful babies."

Kendrea widened her eyes. "You are going to make me choke."

"I have babies on the brain," Lori said wistfully. "I'll be thirty-five in two months and I'm getting broody. Thomas complains about women using him, but he's getting more attention from the opposite sex than me, and I know I'm not unattractive. What gives?"

"Because he goes out and about," Kendrea said. "You practically live in the kitchen here, and then you go next door to your lonely apartment after work. And when you do go out, you glare at the men who compliment you or seem the least bit interested."

"They are supposed to work past the hostility," Lori shrugged. "It's a test to weed out the one-night-stand types."

Kendrea giggled. "And how is that going?"

"It's too early to tell," Lori said. "But I think I found someone. He's a teacher like my dad, and he wears glasses. You know I have a soft spot for a bookish-looking man. Anyway, he's a regular customer here. He's someone I've known for a while. I haven't been encouraging him, but he is persistent."

Kendrea nodded. "If you want love, Lori, stop testing people and start letting them in."

Lori smiled. "And what about you? Are you letting Thomas in?"

Kendrea laughed, but there was a nervous edge to it. "Thomas and I are friends, as you know."

"What I know is that my brother loves you, and he deserves someone who sees him for who he is, not what he looks like or what he can give. And honestly, so do you. It's not as if your relationship choices have been better than his. That skank, Dean Gardener, comes to mind. He broke your heart."

"I wasn't that heartbroken," Kendrea said.

"You two were engaged," Lori said. "You took him to meet the family and everything."

"And then we parted ways," Kendrea shrugged. "It happens. There wasn't even a glaring reason. We just never really meshed. The more we got to know each other, the more we realized it wasn't going to work. I don't want to talk about him; the whole thing was a waste of time."

"Okay," Lori said. "Let's talk about Thomas."

Kendrea sighed. "He said he has a connection with Amanda."

"Rubbish, he's trying to make you jealous," Lori said, a small smile tugging at her lips. "Thomas has only had a connection with you. When are the two of you going to stop playing these games? Sometimes I feel like knocking your heads together and saying, 'Get on with it.' But I know I can't organize your lives, and I have to watch it play out. The truth is, the two of you are exhausting. This Amanda is just a side character in the main drama of your lives."

"Speaking of the side character," Kendrea whistled, "there's her car just driving in. She's late for their meeting."

"You should crash their meeting," Lori said.

"I wouldn't do that," Kendrea frowned.

"Why not?" Lori asked. "Are you planning to save my brother from her, or what?"

"I don't want to interfere in Thomas' love life," Kendrea grinned. "But I am not above creating problems for Amanda. She was an absolute terror in high school. She doesn't deserve to drop in on Thomas a couple of years later and act like she's some goody-two-shoes. She was the one who coined the term Dumbfat. Thomas hated that nickname with a passion."

"Exactly, go," Lori said. "Reach his office first; give Amanda hell."

"But I haven't finished my lunch," Kendrea protested.

"I'll pack your leftovers. When they're done, come back and report to me."

Kendrea chuckled. "Okay. I'm going."

Chapter Five

"You made me late," Amanda scowled at Stephanie, "and now I can't find a parking space, which will make me even more late. Being punctual is professional, and we need this gig."

Stephanie blew a bubble with the gum she was chewing and shrugged. "From what you said about this guy, he's a softie—putty in our hands. What are we stressing about?"

Amanda groaned. "Steph, stop acting nonchalant. Thomas Sterling is the equivalent of a lottery ticket. He's wealthy and good-natured. We will not mess this up. When we're done here, I'll be Mrs. Amanda Sterling. I'll be able to afford a lifestyle we're not accustomed to."

Steph chuckled.

"Stop laughing. You're the one that got us into this mess," Amanda said. "You're the reason why we're back here in Jamaica hustling with barely two cents to rub together."

Stephanie rolled her eyes. "It wasn't all my fault. Your

work permit expired, and you didn't renew it. How am I to blame?"

"You're a U.S. citizen. You were supposed to file for me," Amanda growled. "Sometimes I wish Jed was my father and not yours."

Stephanie laughed. "You can't be serious. Our mother divorced Jed for a reason and ran back to Jamaica, hiding from him for years. Your father was a good, honest man, whom I loved and wished he was my own. So never ever say you would prefer Jed as your father."

"Okay, already, I take it back." Amanda mumbled.

"Besides, I did everything required to file for you. You were supposed to renew your permit. I told you filing for you could take up to ten years. But did you listen? No, you didn't. And here I am, aren't I? I left my job to help you out with your new business venture. Where's the gratitude?"

"You didn't leave your job. You were fired," Amanda snorted.

"Technically, I wasn't fired. I was asked to leave, and they paid me severance to keep my mouth shut. When your boss pushes his hand up your skirt, and you punch him in the face, breaking his nose, nobody wants that to get out."

"That was unnecessary violence," Amanda murmured. "You could have just let it go, kept your job."

"You are crazy. I am not staying around a sexual predator for no job. I would punch him again," Stephanie said. "I only followed you out here because I wanted a change of scenery."

"And you liked my business idea," Amanda said.

"That too," Stephanie nodded. "But you're so high-strung and such a diva, and our entrepreneurship journey has turned into a manhunt."

"It's not a manhunt." Amanda narrowed her eyes at her

sister. "Call it future fiscal planning. I don't want to be in this broke situation again. I hate it."

"I know," Stephanie nodded. "I do too. But from what you told me, this Thomas guy is already halfway smitten, isn't he? You've got this."

"Halfway isn't good enough," Amanda worried. "He needs to fall head over heels—completely and utterly. In the process, I will mold him into the perfect specimen of a man. He has the basic bones for it. Right now, he looks like an overstuffed pillow, but I'm confident that I can make him into a lean, muscular specimen of a man that will make me the envy of all the women on this side of the hemisphere."

Stephanie nodded. "And I will make sure that I cook the healthiest and most nutritious meals for you to accomplish your goals."

Amanda smiled. "You are the best at what you do. That Wellness Spa lost their best chef."

"They did," Stephanie said. "I consoled myself with the thought that people will see a drop in quality and petition for me to come back. And in my fantasies, I'll tell HR, 'Hell to the no.'"

Amanda chuckled. "Ah, here's a parking space." She drove into the recently vacated spot and inhaled. "We're a bit late, but I'm sure it will be fine. Thomas isn't a stickler about anything, really. He's as laid back and accommodative as anyone you'll ever meet. I'll introduce you, and then we'll discuss meals and nutrition. Let me take the lead with this."

"Right," Stephanie nodded. "Only speak when necessary. You're the boss. I get it."

"Good," Amanda nodded.

"But when can we move into his fancy house?" Stephanie said. "I will die if I have to stay with Aunt Gem and the hundred kids for another week."

"You will not die," Amanda snorted. "It could be worse; we could be homeless. And Aunt Gem did give us one of her cars—be grateful."

"Have an attitude of gratitude," Stephanie repeated somberly.

Amanda chuckled, then took one last look at herself in the car mirror and hissed. "What is she doing here?"

"Who?" Steph raised an eyebrow. "Your reflection? That's what happens when you look into mirrors."

"I know, stupid," Amanda hissed. "I'm talking about her, the girl in the black pantsuit heading towards the Deals and Wheels building."

"Wow, nice shape," Stephanie said enviously. "I've always admired that shape—slim yet curvy. She can wear anything and basically look like a million bucks. Who is she?"

"Thomas's gatekeeper. Her name is Kendrea."

Kendrea stopped and turned briefly in their direction before opening the door to the store.

"Oh my, she's pretty," Steph whistled. "How is it that Thomas has a pretty gatekeeper? I thought you said he was basically an overweight simpleton who had developed a crush on you. Why have a crush on you when he has her? You're not that pretty. That girl is seriously above average in looks."

"Shut up," Amanda hissed. "You won't be admiring her when you hear how protective she is of Thomas. She could be the one to ruin our plans."

"Okay, so what's the story?" Steph asked.

"Potted version, because I have to hurry," Amanda said. "I was a mean girl in high school—me, Rachelle, and Kyra. We were in our little clique and benign by and large, but when we got to third form, Thomas was there. They made him repeat third form twice because he had a learning disability.

He was two years older than us, and fat."

"He largely kept to himself and didn't talk to anyone else. He just stared, especially at me, out of his little beady eyes. I developed a revulsion toward him."

"He probably liked you," Stephanie said. "That's why he stared."

"No, it wasn't an adoring look," Amanda shook her head. "He reminded me of Bobby Cassidy, the boy who used to live beside us on Duke Street."

"The boy who sat on you and farted when you were six because you were teasing him?" Stephanie chuckled.

"That's the one, that big blubberous buffoon." Amanda nodded. "I almost died. He could have suffocated me to death. It wasn't funny. Anyway, Thomas's unfortunate resemblance to Bobby made me hate him, so I teased him. Sometimes I made him cry."

"Good Lord, are you sure he has forgiven you?" Stephanie asked. "Maybe this is a trap?"

"Yes, I'm sure," Amanda nodded. "Thomas is a rare person. He doesn't seem to hold a grudge."

"If you say so," Stephanie murmured. "What about the pretty girl, his gatekeeper?"

"Now she does not forget," Amanda said. "My meeting with her was quite testy."

"So, how did she treat him in high school?" Stephanie asked.

"She befriended him," Amanda said. "Wrote his notes and ate lunch with him. They had their own little friend group going. People loved Kendrea, and she had many friends. Because of that, nobody else bothered to trouble Thomas— just me and my friends."

"Kendrea, as you can see, is quite pretty, and all the boys liked her, including a guy that Kyra liked. That's when we kicked it up a notch. Kyra took out her jealousy, not on Kendrea, but on her friend, Thomas. She knew teasing Thomas would rile up Kendrea, and she was right. Rach and I both joined in, and we didn't stop until graduation."

"So, for two years, you tortured Thomas?" Steph shook her head. "Stupid kids."

"I know," Amanda inhaled. "Sometimes we do unfortunate things when we're younger that we sorely regret in the bright glare of adulthood."

"What kind of learning disability does Thomas have?" Steph asked.

"I think it's dysgraphia," Amanda said. "That's the one where you have difficulty writing clearly so others can understand. I remember them allowing him to do his exams on a computer and his homework on a recorder. It took them a while to figure out how to work with him. He wasn't stupid—just unable to write so his teachers could understand what he wrote. Of course, we didn't know that, so we teased him and called him Dumbfat."

"Wow," Stephanie said, shaking her head. "So, you were basically the villain in this story, huh? And now you want to turn him into your project? Bold move."

Amanda scowled. "It's not like that. People change. I've changed. Besides, I'm doing this for him as much as for myself. He needs someone to help him reach his potential—someone who can guide him and bring out his best. When I met him at the wedding a few weeks ago and told him I'm a health and fitness coach with great results, he was so eager for my help. He said he just needed to feel like a normal person and not a circus freak."

"Oh, the poor guy," Stephanie said sympathetically. "Apart from the fact that you have a diet and nutrition degree, are you sure you can help him? After hearing his story, I don't think I'm comfortable with you targeting this man."

"Of course, I can help. I interned at the Mayo Clinic. I've been on teams where we brought down the weight of much heavier people than Thomas," Amanda replied with a wave of her hand. "The point is, I'll make his life better. And mine, too. Now, stay focused. If Kendrea decides she doesn't want Thomas to work with us, she'll shut this down before I can even get started."

Stephanie glanced at the store entrance where Kendrea had disappeared. "Do you think she knows what you're up to?"

"She suspects everything," Amanda muttered. "She's always been protective of him. Back in school, she'd stand up for him like a pit bull. The only reason she didn't come after us harder was because Thomas begged her not to. She's loyal to a fault. But that loyalty might work to my advantage."

Stephanie raised an eyebrow. "How do you figure that?"

"If I can convince her that I've turned over a new leaf, that I'm here to genuinely help Thomas, she might lower her guard. Once she's on my side, she'll pave the way for me, and then I can be with Thomas."

"That's a lot of ifs," Stephanie pointed out.

Amanda smirked. "Watch and learn, big sister. Watch and learn."

They stepped out of the car, Amanda straightening her dress and flipping her hair back with practiced ease. She strode toward the Deals and Wheels building, exuding confidence, with Stephanie trailing behind her.

As they reached the door, Stephanie leaned closer and whispered, "What if Kendrea doesn't buy this new and improved professional version of you?"

Amanda didn't miss a beat. "Then we'll cross that bridge

when we get to it. But trust me, Stephanie. I always get what I want."

Stephanie shook her head but couldn't suppress a small grin. "This is going to be entertaining if nothing else."

Amanda pushed the door open, her polished smile firmly in place, as they walked into the building to begin their mission.

Chapter Six

Thomas was having a more maddening day than usual. He had started late because he had stayed up until the wee hours with heartburn, and then he had the brilliant idea of using ice cream to soothe it.

That was a bad idea. It had made it worse. He had sat down in the middle of his living room in the half-dark and watched as the rays of the morning sun peeped over the horizon. Then, he had come to the realization that he was tired of living like he was. He had fallen asleep in his living room, feeling depressed and disheartened about his eating habits. He had to give himself a pep talk to drag himself out of bed at ten.

He was thankful his office was just downstairs and that he had put in an elevator to take him there whenever the whim struck him. He had formal meetings, but most of the time, he worked from his two-bedroom apartment, where he traded stocks, played video games, and ordered takeout when he was hungry.

Sometimes, the only person he saw was his housekeeper, Noreen, who came in three times a week, and she knew to leave him alone. Even though he had heard her whisper more than once that this was no way for a grown man to live, implying that something was wrong with his lifestyle, he didn't really care.

All his business interests were booming. He had taken his inheritance and multiplied it a hundredfold. He hired good people to run his various businesses, which meant he didn't have to be present for the day-to-day running of any of his ventures.

He checked his email daily, though. Patti, the secretary he shared with Brian, the manager of Deals on Wheels, usually handled his day-to-day correspondence and arranged his mail according to priority. In the priority section, he saw a legal notice, which copied him and his lawyer, Camden Byfield. The subject was: Notice of Legal Action Regarding Commercial Property. He started reading.

Dear Mr. Sterling,

I am writing on behalf of my client, Ms. Nicole Pink, regarding the recent dispute over her use of the commercial property at Beach Cove Plaza.

As you are aware, Ms. Pink has operated her business at this property for an extended period, relying on the understanding that you had granted her permission to do so under a clear agreement, even if not formalized in writing. Specifically, my client asserts that the arrangement included a verbal agreement allowing her to use the space for at least two years without rent as part of your mutual understanding during your relationship.

By requesting that she vacate the premises prematurely, you

have breached this agreement, which has caused significant disruption to her business operations. Consequently, my client has initiated legal proceedings to address this matter and seek appropriate remedies.

To resolve this matter efficiently and avoid further escalation, we are open to engaging in discussions before proceeding further with litigation.

Should you wish to resolve the issue outside of court, I encourage you to have your legal counsel contact me directly by December 10. If we do not hear from you by then, we will proceed with the case as filed.

Please understand that this email is not intended to be adversarial but to outline my client's position and extend an opportunity for dialogue.

Sincerely,

Alan Byfield, Attorney at Law

Alan Byfield was her new boyfriend, apparently. Thomas read through the document again slowly in utter disbelief. She was suing him—for asking her to vacate the commercial property she'd been occupying rent-free for months. Could she even do that?

Thomas leaned back in his chair and let out a heavy sigh. It wasn't just the absurdity of her argument that got to him— it was the gall. Nicole knew full well that he'd only let her use the space as a favor when they were together. There had been no talk of formal terms, no promises made. But now, here she was, twisting things into something they weren't.

That property was the only reason she had dated him in the first place. She had wanted a prime location to house her clothing business, since he had just bought Beach Cove Shopping Center in the heart of the tourist mecca. She had done her research, swallowed her revulsion, and dated him.

Deep down, he had known she was only using him, and yet he had allowed her to do it.

They had been together for almost a year, and not once had she gone out in public with him. If her friend had not recorded that conversation, and he hadn't heard what she actually thought about him, he would still be with her, being used.

To be fair and honest, he had used her too. Twice a week, she came to his apartment, and they had sex. It had felt transactional, but he didn't quibble about it. At least she wasn't a prostitute.

He had tried that before—never again. The words cold and clinical came to mind, and he didn't feel satisfied afterward.

At least Nicole had provided a welcome distraction from his loneliness, which was a constant companion. She had attempted conversation and pretended to listen to him. What more could a guy ask for?

Nicole came into his life when Kendrea was seeing Dean Gregory. He always made his worst relationship decisions when Kendrea had a boyfriend or was dating. First, he went into a deep depression and became more withdrawn than usual. Then, he had relationships with women like Nicole.

The ringing of his personal phone jolted him out of his ruminations. He expected it to be Amanda; he had a meeting with her, and she was late. But it wasn't Amanda—it was his lawyer, Camden Byfield.

"I saw the email," Camden said after they greeted each other.

"Their case is laughable," Thomas said tiredly. "The truth is, while Nicole and I were together, I allowed her to stay rent-free at one of the shops. We broke up, and she didn't pay any rent for three months, so I instructed my business manager to start charging her rent. Now she has the brilliant idea to sue me. Does she think I'm that much of a pushover?"

"Their case is weak," Camden agreed. "Nonverbal agreements, especially ones without any supporting documentation, rarely hold up in court. She'll have to prove that such an agreement existed, and given the circumstances, that's a tall order."

Thomas leaned back in his chair, frustration bubbling under his calm exterior. "It's not just the lawsuit that bothers me—it's the principle. She used me, Camden. And now she's trying to bleed me dry. What's the matter with people these days? I've been more than generous, especially considering the circumstances around our breakup."

"How did that go again?" Camden asked.

"She told her friend, Abby, who so happens to be a cousin of mine, that she was only with me for the perks. Abby had accidentally recorded the conversation. When she found out that she did, she sent it to me. I broke up with Nicole the very next day, and I allowed her to stay in my building for three months after the breakup without charging her rent. That was generous of me, wasn't it?"

"It was," Camden said. "You were generous. This sounds like it can be resolved quickly. I'll prepare the response and counter any claims they make with evidence. If she's been there rent-free for this long without a lease or agreement, it's easy to establish that she was a guest at best, not a tenant with rights to the property."

Thomas pinched the bridge of his nose, trying to push back the throbbing headache forming. "Just make it go away, Camden. I've already wasted enough time and energy on her."

"We'll take care of it," Camden assured him. "I'll reach out to her lawyer to schedule a meeting; he'll drop the case after our talk. I am his boss, after all."

"What are they dating now?" Thomas said snarkily. "Does Alan Byfield know that I'm a major client of your firm? Why did he take her case?"

"He knows," Camden said. "He must be losing his mind. Taking her case would be a conflict of interest if there was anything to it. I'll resolve this shortly. Trust me. I'll keep you posted."

"Thanks, Camden. I appreciate it," Thomas said, his voice weary.

After ending the call, Thomas sat in silence, staring into space. Nicole had been good for one thing—she had hurt and humiliated him into doing something about his situation. Not that he hadn't been toying with the idea of losing weight and feeling different before, but her conversation with Abby had been the kick in the seat of his pants that he needed. He thought about the conversation Nicole had with Abby and squeezed the stress ball on his table. Just one statement from her had been enough to wake him up.

"I like Thomas and all, but he probably weighs the same as my father's prize pig, Franco. And though he's a nice, kind man who gives me whatever I ask for, his obesity is a big turn-off. That won't stop me from milking him dry, though. And I'll milk him until he can't be milked anymore. I should think of him as a cow instead of a pig. A cash cow."

"Does he know that you think that?" Abby gasped.

"No, he doesn't," Nicole snorted. "I'm a good actress, the best. I'll even marry him if he asks and have his children to tie me to his legacy. He may be fat, but he's not bad in bed. Listen, I figure that he's so fat that he may not be long for this world. Surely his poor heart will give way soon. All that fat and bad lifestyle will surely do him in someday soon, and when he goes, all his wealth will be mine. Come to think of it, that's not a bad outcome."

Thomas leaned back in his chair, now fully awake. Nicole's assertions about his longevity had woken him up like nothing else could have. At first, it had caused him to derail a bit. He had sunk his emotions into food for a few months after the breakup, but now, he was ready to lose the weight, the old-fashioned way—no weight loss medication or surgery for him. He had considered the side effects of both and didn't want to contemplate any of it. His mother had died in the middle of a routine dental surgery. He didn't want to go through anything like that unless he absolutely had to.

Meeting Amanda again had been a godsend. He was in the right mindset now to lose weight. He was frankly tired of his old favorite foods—they weren't giving him the joy they once had. Heartburn was now his constant companion.

Besides, he wasn't opposed to exercising—pushing his body to limits and feeling the burn, like his friend Griffin was always talking about. Maybe now he could participate in their Thursday night basketball games. They always invited him, and he never showed up. How could he? Walking a short distance made him pant, much less running up and down a court.

And wouldn't it be nice if he could be the object of adoration instead of pity to the opposite sex? All the women he was interested in inevitably had that look of pity in their eyes when they stared at him. Even the women who were as big as he was. It was a look of revulsion mixed with pity. It usually mellowed into something more when he tried on the charm and they realized he wasn't broke, but that initial look was always there. It showed up like clockwork.

Everybody except Kendrea had it. She always looked at him with warmth and fondness.

He had been withdrawn when he first met her in high

school. He knew he looked older than the new batch of students and had gained twenty pounds over the summer. He had been withdrawn because of humiliation of being kept back two years because of his atrocious handwriting. He could read well, but his writing made it impossible for him to communicate that he had absorbed all the material taught to him. It had taken them two years to figure out how to work with him.

Everybody had just labeled him the fat, dumb kid and stayed away from him as if he was contagious. But Kendrea had defended him and treated him like a person.

He didn't care what role she was in his life; he just knew he wanted her there and never wanted to lose her.

"Knock, knock." Kendrea pushed her head around the door. "Your secretary said you weren't busy."

"Oh yes," Thomas smiled. "I'm supposed to be meeting Amanda."

"She's late," Kendrea said, coming further into his office. "I saw her in the parking lot trying to find a place to park."

Kendrea was in a pantsuit that molded her curves effortlessly, her face flawless as usual, her brown skin glowing. He had always thought Kendrea had doll-like features with her perfectly symmetrical face, full lips, and those large, expressive eyes that seemed to hold the secrets of the universe. Her hair was pulled back into a sleek bun, exposing the graceful curve of her neck. Thomas felt the familiar pang of admiration mixed with longing as he took her in. Her silky blouse was open just enough to show her necklace: T heart K. It stood for "Thomas loves Kendrea." He had bought her that necklace four years ago and given it to her on Valentine's Day. She always wore it. He wondered if she knew how it made him feel that she cherished his gift—and that he really meant it. He loved her. He always would. Nobody even came close.

She sat across from him and looked around. "You redecorated and didn't tell me?"

"I did," Thomas nodded. "Lorraine Byfield, your old boss, did it. She decorated downstairs, and I told her to overhaul the offices."

"It's nice," Kendrea said. "She's the best commercial interior designer there is."

"I said the same thing when I saw it first," Thomas said. "I would have asked you to do it, but you were busy."

"I was. Still am," Kendrea sighed. "I'm going to need to hire help. I've put out some feelers and have a good prospect."

"Expansion after a year," Thomas smiled. "That's good. That's progress."

"I know, and it's all because of you," Kendrea chuckled. "That Chamber of Commerce dinner keeps on giving. I'll also rent office space close to you when Yasmin's building is finished. I'll be right next door to you."

"So we'll live together and work in the same place," Thomas said softly. "I like that."

Kendrea smiled. "Maybe it won't be fun if we have a fight."

"We'll be fine," Thomas smiled. "What brings you here at this time of the day?"

"Hunger," she replied. "My client pushed back the meeting time. I just had lunch with Lori and thought I'd come and see what you were up to."

"Nothing much," Thomas said. "Just thinking about the past and my readiness to lose the weight."

"I'm so proud of you," Kendrea said. "I don't know who is responsible for your newfound determination, but I like it."

Thomas smiled sadly. "The conversation with Nicole and

Abby was a kick in the pants."

"Nicole?" Kendrea sneered. "I didn't like her one bit. You could see the phoniness a mile away."

"I didn't see it," Thomas sighed. "I actually thought there was a girl who treats me like you do."

"And how is that?" Kendrea frowned.

"Like a human being with feelings," Thomas said. "In the world of romance, my feelings are not respected. I'm just a means to an end. I thought I had gotten used to it, but Nicole was a really good actress when she was with me."

Kendrea winced. "I'm amazed she didn't try to have your baby. It's the lucrative thing to do."

"I always wear protection," Thomas said. "I'm not that gullible. I know about the eighteen-year plan. Besides, the only person I want to have children with is you... after we get married, of course."

Kendrea frowned. "I don't take you seriously when you say things like that."

"Why not?" Thomas asked.

"Because you say it, and then the next thing I know, you have a girlfriend."

"Only after you get a boyfriend," Thomas said. "I thought you'd recognize the pattern by now. When you start dating someone, you have no time for me, so I try to do my own thing too. Can you blame me?"

"I don't have a boyfriend now," Kendrea said. "And yet you have Amanda."

"Amanda is to help me with my weight loss," Thomas said. "You will always be the love of my life."

His phone rang before she could answer, and he was somewhat relieved. He didn't want to hear her routine answer: that she didn't love him like he did her and that he was just her best friend. It was their thing—he told her he loved her and wanted to marry her, and she shot him down.

"Mr. Sterling, Miss Amanda Pierce and her sister, Miss Stephanie Williams, are here to see you."

"Oh, send them in," Thomas said.

He looked at Kendrea. "Are you staying for the meeting?"

Kendrea nodded. "Oh yes. I want to know if Amanda is just another gold digger or if she knows what she's about."

Chapter Seven

"**I** am so sorry I'm late," Amanda said breathlessly as she walked through the door. She looked at Thomas and then at Kendrea. Her eyes dimmed slightly when she saw Kendrea there.

Kendrea subdued a chuckle.

"It's no problem, Amanda," Thomas said pleasantly. "My attention was taken up with something else, too."

"Oh, that's a relief," Amanda said. "Is Kendrea going to sit in on the meeting?"

Kendrea nodded. "I have a couple of minutes until I meet my next client. I may not stay for all of it. I'll try not to interfere—I know this is your wheelhouse."

"Have a seat," Thomas said, pointing to the vacant chairs before his desk.

"Oh, yes," Amanda said. "Thank you. I would like to introduce you to Stephanie Williams; she will be your chef."

"Hello," Stephanie said as she stepped out from behind

Amanda and greeted them. She was a chunkier, less attractive version of Amanda and appeared shy. They were obviously related.

Kendrea watched with narrowed eyes as they took their seats. Amanda's body language screamed disapproval of Kendrea's presence.

If it was driving Amanda crazy, and Kendrea loved it. She wanted to be mature and adult about this arrangement, but she couldn't shake the memory of Amanda's sneering face from high school.

Amanda had apologized and said she was an idiot, but Kendrea was still suspicious. She shifted her gaze to Thomas, who was looking at Amanda with a pleasant expression. How did he do it? How did he forgive all the vicious things people said about him and still give them the time of day?

I couldn't do it. Kendrea thought darkly. If people had attacked her the way they did Thomas, she doubted she'd ever smile again—or even get out of bed in the mornings. She would hate the world.

"This meeting is personal," Amanda said. "As your health and fitness coach, I'll need to know specific details about your eating and exercise habits to tailor a program. If you're uncomfortable with either Stephanie or, um, Kendrea being privy to some details, we can always ask them to leave."

"Kendrea knows everything about me. Maybe she should be the one you're interviewing," Thomas said with a shrug. He glanced at his watch. "Let's get to it, Amanda. I have a shareholders' meeting to prep for, and I'll need time to look over some numbers."

"Oh, er, well then," Amanda stammered, looking down at her notes, clearly flustered. Thomas wasn't fawning over her like a lovestruck kitten, and he'd made it clear Kendrea was an important part of his life.

Kendrea hid a smirk.

"Well," Amanda said, regaining her composure. "Let's start with the basics. Thomas, could you walk me through a typical day's meals and exercise habits?" She pulled out a sleek tablet and stylus, her fingers trembling slightly as she tapped the screen.

Thomas leaned back in his chair, his expression neutral but faintly amused. "Sure," he said. "Breakfast is usually black coffee and a protein bar. Lunch is hit or miss—sometimes whatever is on special at the Korean Fusion restaurant next door or whichever fast-food place I pass if I'm on the road. Dinner? That's a rotation of takeout menus, depending on what I'm in the mood for. Last night, it was hot wings, barbecued ribs, and fried fish with extra vinegar. I ended up with heartburn all night."

Stephanie gasped. "You ate all that in one go?"

"I did," Thomas said, "unfortunately, all of that spice did not agree with me, and I ate some ice cream to calm the fires raging in my gut; I ended up writhing on the living room couch in pain until my over-the-counter medication kicked in.

Kendrea shook her head. "Typical."

"As for exercise," Thomas shrugged, "If you call walking to the refrigerator exercise I do that a lot. I eat when I feel stressed, which, lately, is often."

Amanda frowned slightly, scribbling on her tablet. "That's… not the most balanced routine. We'll need to make adjustments."

"Lots of adjustments." Thomas agreed. "I told my doctor that you wanted a report on my current health in order to help and she mentioned that she was thinking about having a health and fitness coach on her staff. She said you should call her when your time with me is up and she said she appreciated your detailed questionnaire. She even made some additional notes for you on the back."

"Oh, that's lovely," Amanda smiled.

Thomas handed her the document. "By the way, I think her scale is wrong."

Kendrea snickered.

Thomas laughed with her, "I bet you wouldn't guess how much I am weighing at the moment, Drea."

"Mmm," Kendrea looked at him, "definitely over three hundred."

"Three hundred and ten at six feet tall and with a body fat percentage of thirty-six percent," Thomas finished with a wry smile. "My doctor gave me a pretty blunt rundown during my last visit. She said I'm officially in the danger zone and need to make serious changes."

Stephanie gasped again, her hand flying to her mouth. "Oh my! That sounds... alarming."

Thomas shrugged nonchalantly. "It's not news to me. I've been feeling it—less energy, harder to focus. I know I've let things slide, but with everything going on, it's just easier to eat away my feelings than deal with them."

Amanda's frown deepened as she reviewed the document he handed her. "Well, Thomas, you're not alone. These habits didn't form overnight, and it's going to take some time to replace them with healthier ones. But the good news is, you're willing to do the work, right?"

"Depends," Thomas said, smirking. "Is this going to involve kale smoothies and 5 a.m. runs?"

"No 5 a.m. runs—at least not yet," Amanda said, "We'll focus on small, manageable changes to build momentum. Stephanie will cook all your meals, so there will be no need for takeout. In fact, it is discouraged for the next six months. All your meals and drinks will come from your kitchen."

Thomas nodded, looking at Stephanie. "You up for the challenge?"

Stephanie nodded. "Of course. I'll make sure your meals are healthy and delicious. I won't serve kale smoothies unless you request them," she said nervously.

Thomas smiled. "Good. And that request will never be made."

Amanda's lips twitched. "So Thomas are you ready for this?"

"Yes," Thomas nodded, "I want to lose the weight. I am finally ready to get this done. My mind is made up. I will work on it under my own steam. I doubt you will find it hard to motivate me. When I make up my mind to do something, it usually gets done. And right now, I want the weight off because I want to be healthy and live long enough to be there for my future wife and children."

He looked at Kendrea significantly and then turned back to Amanda. "I am doing this for myself. I just have one request: Don't tailor a program that will make it hard for me to follow long-term. It has to be a lifestyle change. I have never dieted, and from what I can see from others who have tried it, it doesn't look like fun."

"That's no problem." Amanda said confidently, "We have many tools in our weight loss arsenal. Weight loss can be approached in different ways. We can adjust the timing of your meals, incorporate healthier food choices, and even include some fasting protocols if you're open to that."

Thomas raised an eyebrow. "Fasting? As in skipping meals? That doesn't sound like fun."

"It's not about skipping meals," Amanda clarified, tapping her tablet. "It's about giving your body structured periods to reset and burn stored energy more effectively. For example, intermittent fasting is a popular and research-supported method. It could mean having all your meals within an eight-hour window or skipping breakfast a few days a week."

Thomas frowned. "So... no breakfast? I thought that was the most important meal of the day."

"Not necessarily," Amanda said. "It depends on your body and your goals. Some people find they have better energy levels and focus when they skip breakfast, while others don't. It's not one-size-fits-all. That's why we'll experiment and see what works best for you."

"I guess that doesn't sound so bad," Thomas said reluctantly. A buddy of mine lost a lot of weight fasting, but he regained it all when he started eating normally. When I lose this weight, I don't want to regain any of it."

"I know," Amanda said reassuringly. "That's why our focus won't just be on losing weight, but on creating sustainable habits you can maintain for life. Fasting is just one tool in the toolbox. It's effective for some people, but it's not a magic bullet. We'll pair it with a balanced diet and an exercise routine that works for you."

Thomas nodded slowly. "Okay, but how do I make sure I don't fall back into old habits once I hit my goal? That's what I'm worried about."

"That's a great question," Amanda said, smiling. "The key is to approach this as a lifestyle change, not a temporary fix. We'll focus on building habits that stick—like preparing your own meals, finding physical activities you enjoy, and learning how to manage stress without turning to food. Maintenance is just as important as the weight loss phase."

"And if I slip up?" Thomas asked, leaning forward slightly.

"You will," Amanda said matter-of-factly. "And that's okay. Progress isn't about perfection. It's about consistency over time. When you slip up, we'll reassess, figure out what happened, and get you back on track. No guilt trips, just solutions."

Thomas sat back, thoughtful. "That makes sense."

It really did, Kendrea thought. Her distrust of Amanda slowly melted under her professional responses. Obviously, she was going to be worth the money. Her phone beeped, and she surreptitiously checked it. It was her client, asking if she could meet in thirty minutes.

Of course, she could; Thomas seemed to be in good hands.

"Looks like you've got everything under control, Amanda. I'm curious to see how this pans out." Kendrea said briskly.

Amanda met Kendrea's gaze, her smile tight but polite. "It's a challenge I'm ready for."

Thomas smiled. "Thanks, Amanda. I appreciate the effort you're putting into this."

When can we expect to move into Ridgeview? Amanda asked. The sooner we get going the better.

Thomas looked at Kendrea, "It's up to Kendrea. She has been steadily decorating, and I haven't even seen the place yet."

"You haven't?" Amanda gasped.

"No," Thomas said, "Kendrea assures me it is coming along nicely."

"But it's where you are going to live," Amanda frowned. Don't you care about it?"

"Nope, decorating is Kendrea's business, I trust her implicitly. If she likes it, I love it."

"Must be nice," Amanda muttered under her breath.

Kendrea chuckled. Amanda looked crestfallen. Maybe she thought she would just waltz in and take over Thomas' life—well, not under my watch.

Kendrea said out loud, "Give me a week. I do have to equip the gym. You gave me the plan only today, Amanda. Luckily, my sports goods supplier said he has everything on the list you sent."

"Good." Amanda nodded. "That's great."

"And you should see the progress, Thomas." Kendrea said, getting up, "We'll meet there tomorrow evening. I'll call you with a time. Excuse me, everyone, but my client has pushed up the meeting again."

"Thanks for being here, Kendrea. I'll see you tomorrow evening at Ridgeview." Thomas nodded.

"Looking forward to it. Take care, Thomas. Amanda, Stephanie." She gave them each a polite nod before heading toward the door.

Amanda's polite smile faltered slightly as the door clicked shut behind her. She adjusted her tablet and looked at Thomas. "She's very... involved, isn't she?"

Thomas smiled. "Kendrea and I have been through a lot together. She's not just involved; she's integral. I couldn't ask for a better friend."

Amanda's smile didn't quite reach her eyes. "Of course. The kind of friendship you both have is rare."

"Oh, it is," Thomas said, "and that's why she is moving in with us at Ridgeview through the duration of this healthy journey I am on, I figure I can use all the help I can get."

He missed the look of shock on Amanda's face.

Chapter Eight

Kendrea was exhausted when she arrived home after a long day. She kicked off her shoes and walked into the spacious townhouse. She had been the one to decorate it after her sister, Kenny, bought it. Kenny had put her on a tight budget, but she had done wonders with the place. It was still her favorite project. At the time, she had been interning with Zen Design, Camden's mother's firm. As a rookie, they didn't allow her to work on any project alone. This place had shown her what she was capable of.

She headed for the fridge in the open-plan kitchen and grimaced—she had one sparkling water left. There was no food. She would have to go shopping. She was looking forward to staying with Thomas at Ridgeview and having a personal chef.

Like Thomas, she wasn't fond of cooking. She expressed her creativity on canvas, where she usually did abstract art. She was working on two pieces simultaneously—one as a wedding present for her sister and Camden and the other for Thomas's living room. She wanted to create a giant art piece that would tie the whole room together. His living room had a modern, minimalist vibe with clean lines and muted tones, but Kendrea thought it needed a bold splash of color to bring it to life. She had already sketched out a few ideas—a vibrant interplay of reds, golds, and deep blues that would make the space feel more dynamic without overwhelming its serene atmosphere.

Grabbing the sparkling water, she plopped down on the sleek gray sectional sofa and stretched out, staring at the blank canvas propped against the wall. She was trying to decide whether to incorporate a texture technique she'd recently learned. She smiled, thinking about how Thomas had encouraged her to push her boundaries. He was always supportive, even when she second-guessed herself.

Her phone buzzed on the coffee table, interrupting her thoughts. It was a text from Kenny.

I'm adding one more to the guest list. Don't kill me. It's DJ Duke—he agreed to perform. Squeal!!!

Kendrea groaned. The engagement party kept getting bigger and bigger. She texted back:

That's it. No more. We'll chat tomorrow.

After setting down the phone, Kendrea glanced at the wedding gift canvas again. It needed to be perfect—not just a piece of art but a representation of love, commitment, and all the things she hoped Kenny and Camden would share. Her heart warmed as she thought about how happy her sister had been lately.

But Thomas lingered in her mind too.

How did she really feel about him? She'd been wondering about that more and more. He had no problem declaring his undying love for her, but she had always thought it was just

Thomas being over the top, as usual. She always brushed him off. They were friends. He had been saying he loved her since their early teens. Admittedly, she had always had a soft spot for him, but it wasn't until that Chamber of Commerce dinner that she started thinking about him differently. And once she started, she couldn't stop. It was like it had unlocked the attraction buried deep inside her.

She turned on the television to watch the news recap of the day. She would spend a few minutes catching up, then shower and head to bed. She had to get up early to put the finishing touches on Thomas's canvas. She wanted to take it with her tomorrow when they went to his place.

But her mind kept straying back to that night—the kiss that changed their friendship, at least for her. She turned off the television and closed her eyes to reminisce.

A few months ago…

"You have to help me," Thomas said over the phone in a panic.

"Why?"

When Thomas called, Kendrea had been sitting in her office, staring into space and questioning her life choices. She had made the big move to start her own interior design business, but so far, her list of clients mainly consisted of family connections, pity hires, and small jobs. Meanwhile, the rent for the office space she had leased in a plaza—hoping to appear more official—was looming over her.

So far, she had gotten no walk-in customers.

"Kendrea, why do I feel like you're not listening?" Thomas asked urgently.

"Well, I wasn't," she admitted. "I was thinking about how stupid I was to open a shop before establishing a reputation.

I'm dipping into my savings for nothing." Shaking off her frustration, she refocused. "What do you need help with?"

"I need a date for the Chamber of Commerce dinner," Thomas said. "I kind of hinted to Griffin and the guys that I had a hot date. At the time, I was thinking of Nicole, but as you know, we've since broken up."

"Oh yes," Kendrea murmured. "Nicole—the user—who compared you to a pig, said she would milk you dry and was hoping for you to die early. That Nicole?"

"Yes," Thomas hissed. "I wish I never sent you that conversation. How long are you going to gloat about being right?"

"I don't know," Kendrea mused. "I could do this all year."

"Well, are you willing to come with me and help me save face?" Thomas sounded genuinely panicked.

She grinned. "What's in it for me?"

"Access to the town's movers and shakers—a couple of hotels, Airbnb, and guesthouse owners, property developers, and rich people who need their houses designed from time to time."

"When is it?" Kendrea sat up in her chair.

"Tomorrow," Thomas laughed. "I already dropped a few words here and there for you, smoothed your way a little. You should especially talk to Richard Tinsdale—he said he has a couple of houses he wants staged and a few short-term rentals that need work."

"Ooooh." Kendrea was almost drooling. Richard Tinsdale would be a huge client. Her sister, Kenny, had even designed an app for him.

Thomas chuckled. "Not to mention, Larry Nelson said some of the houses Nelson Construction is building in Pleasant View Hills are ready for interior design. You could get in on his team."

"That would be awesome," Kendrea breathed. "You've been looking out for me."

"Always," Thomas said. "You wanted to do this on your own, but everybody needs a leg up when they're just starting out."

"I'll be your date," Kendrea said, her heart melting. She shouldn't have given him such a hard time—he had been so kind—but she was still mad at him for ignoring her warnings about Nicole.

"Tomorrow night. The dress code is formal. I'll pick you up," Thomas said triumphantly.

****

Kendrea was surprised at how good Thomas looked in a tux. When she first saw him, his large midsection was somewhat contained, he was clean-shaven, and he appeared taller and more stately. He had come to collect her in one of his newest cars—a sleek black Toyota Land Cruiser.

His face broke into a wide grin when he opened the passenger door.

"You look gorgeous. Red is definitely your color," he said, his voice filled with open admiration.

Usually, that kind of adoration from Thomas was par for the course, but when she brushed past him to slide into the car, something shifted. Her heart stuttered slightly, especially when his fingers lightly grazed her leg as he adjusted the hem of her dress. Then she caught a whiff of his cologne. The sudden urge to bury her face in his jacket and just breathe him in left her momentarily unsteady.

What on earth was wrong with her?

"You clean up well yourself," Kendrea replied, her voice not quite as steady as she'd like. Her heart raced as if this were the first time she was seeing Thomas.

The night didn't get any easier.

It was as if her body had suddenly tuned in to him in a way it never had before. She was hyper-aware of every casual touch, every deep rumble of his voice, every glance he sent her way.

The Chamber of Commerce had rented out the Montego Bay Convention Center for the event, and the venue was breathtaking. Elegant floral arrangements, shimmering table linens, and soft ambient lighting created a luxurious atmosphere. The theme for the night, Building Bridges to Prosperity, was reflected in arching structures and intricate centerpieces symbolizing unity and growth.

As Kendrea stepped inside with Thomas by her side, she couldn't shake the strange fluttering in her chest. She had attended countless events with him before, but tonight felt different.

Maybe it was the way his hand rested lightly on her back as they maneuvered through the crowd. Or the way his deep voice resonated when he introduced her to the first group of people they met.

Thomas' best friend, Griffin, approached with his fiancée, Tracy. They made a striking couple—Griffin tall and muscular, Tracy petite and effortlessly pretty.

"Why aren't you coming to the wedding?" Tracy asked playfully. "The twins would love to see you."

Kendrea laughed. "The last time I went to an event with your brothers, they had a fight over who I liked more—which was crazy because I can't even tell them apart. Sorry about the wedding, though. It's on the same day as the interior design expo. I already wrangled some showpieces from a few brands, and I'm hoping it drums up some business."

"I understand." Tracy squeezed her arm reassuringly. "It's

okay. Actually, it was Griffin's mom who wanted it on a Wednesday. She's only able to come to Jamaica two days before and has to leave the day after."

"I'll be there," Thomas said.

"You have to be—you're the best man," Griffin reminded him with a playful elbow to the ribs.

Kendrea smiled as she watched them. Griffin, Thomas, and their other childhood friend, Malik, had been inseparable since kindergarten. Griffin often joked that he knew Thomas back when he was skinny.

Thomas started packing on weight by age eight so that was a long time ago.

After chatting with the couple for a bit, Thomas led Kendrea away to mingle.

That's when she saw him in his element. Confident. Charismatic. Effortlessly shaking hands and exchanging easy banter with the town's elite.

She watched him more than she intended, noticing details she had somehow overlooked before—like how his smile lit up his entire face or how intently he listened when others spoke.

"Are you okay?" Thomas leaned in close, his warm breath brushing against her ear. The proximity made her stomach flip.

"Yes," Kendrea replied quickly, her voice a little higher than she intended. "Just... taking it all in."

He grinned, his eyes crinkling at the corners. "Stick close to me, and I'll make sure you meet everyone you need to."

True to his word, Thomas was a master at making connections. Kendrea was introduced to some key people who were just as influential as Thomas had promised.

She had a long conversation with a popular interior designer, Janet Cohen, who waxed poetic about her early days starting out. She was both encouraging and helpful. Kendrea could barely contain her excitement as she exchanged contact information with the woman, who promised to send some business her way because she was so swamped.

"Now, now—if it isn't Kendrea the gorgeous."

She heard the familiar voice behind her just after finishing her conversation with Janet.

Spinning around, she found herself face-to-face with her ex, Dean Gardener. He was looking as handsome as ever, wearing his signature sly grin and an impeccably tailored suit. Dean had always been effortlessly charming, and tonight was no exception. He was the definition of tall, dark, and handsome, with his rich, coffee-toned skin and piercing amber eyes that always seemed to hold a hint of mischief. His clean-shaven face and perfectly groomed hair completed the polished look he was known for. Dean had a presence that demanded attention, and as much as Kendrea hated to admit it, he hadn't lost his touch.

"Dean," she said, keeping her tone neutral and her expression composed. "I didn't expect to see you here tonight."

"Well, you know me," he replied, flashing that infamous grin. "I always show up where it matters. And it seems I made the right choice—running into you."

Kendrea crossed her arms loosely, a subtle barrier she hoped would communicate the boundaries she needed. "Still as smooth as ever, I see."

Dean chuckled, his laugh low and familiar. "And you're still as stunning as always. What's it been, two years?"

"Eighteen months," Kendrea corrected without hesitation, her gaze steady.

"Time flies," Dean said, his tone tinged with something

she couldn't quite place—nostalgia, regret? Whatever it was, she didn't care.

"So, tell me, Kendrea. How's life treating you? You look like you're thriving."

"I am," Kendrea replied with a polite smile. "Work's keeping me busy. Why are you in Montego Bay?"

"Wouldn't you know it? I was laid off from my job in Kingston, so I returned home and decided to do my own thing. I bought a cellphone business about six months ago, and it's been going well. Seeing you here is just the icing on the cake. You look amazing, as always."

"Thank you," Kendrea replied politely, but she stepped back slightly, creating a bit more space between them. "How have you been?"

"Busy, but good," Dean said, his eyes flicking briefly to Thomas, who had just reappeared at Kendrea's side. "And you? Seems like you're doing well for yourself business-wise, rubbing shoulders with the successful Thomas Sterling."

"She is," Thomas interjected smoothly, his tone calm but firm as he extended a hand toward Dean. "Dean Gardener, how are you?"

"Great," Dean said with a smile. "There has to be a secret to you two being friends this long. I mean, have you two done the deed yet? I can't imagine having a girl as hot as Kendrea and not wanting to, you know…"

Kendrea felt her jaw tighten, but Thomas let out a short, humorless laugh before she could say a word.

"That's an interesting assumption," Thomas said, his grip on Dean's hand tightening just a fraction before he let go. "But some of us know how to value friendships without making everything about sex."

Dean smirked, clearly unfazed. "Hey, I'm just saying what

everyone's probably thinking. You two have been tight for years. No way there hasn't been at least a little something-something going on."

"Oh, there's Richard Tinsdale—I have to see him," Kendrea said smoothly, cutting the conversation short. "It was nice catching up, but we should keep mingling. Lots of people to meet tonight."

"Of course," Dean said, his grin returning as he stepped aside. "Don't be a stranger, Kendrea."

They walked in Richard's direction, but Thomas stopped her once they were some distance away from Dean.

"I never liked that guy."

Kendrea chuckled. "I know. You've said it several times."

"I almost single-handedly derailed my life because of him," Thomas sighed.

"Why?" Kendrea asked softly.

"Because you said you loved him," Thomas said. "I could handle your physical relationship with him, but I couldn't handle your declaration of love or the fact that you were engaged or that you proudly introduced him as your fiancé two years ago."

"Thomas..." Kendrea looked up at him, her heart doing that annoying fluttering thing again. "Dean is the past. We are living in the now."

Thomas held her gaze, his expression unreadable for a moment before a small, rueful smile appeared. "I know that," he said softly. "But sometimes, the past has a way of sneaking into the present, doesn't it?"

Kendrea frowned, unsure how to respond. She placed a hand lightly on his arm. "It doesn't matter, Thomas. Not to me. Not anymore. Dean is... ancient history."

"Good," Thomas replied, his voice low and steady. "Because he doesn't get to walk back into your life and stir things up. Not when you've come so far."

Kendrea studied him carefully, noticing the flicker of protectiveness in his expression. She knew Thomas had always been there for her—through bad breakups, career struggles, and personal growth. But this conversation felt like it was brushing the edges of something unspoken between them, something that made her pulse quicken.

"Let's get back to the event," she said, her voice softening. "We're here to celebrate and network, not to let old ghosts haunt us."

Thomas's smile turned warm and reassuring. "You're right, as always." He extended his arm to her. "Shall we?"

Kendrea looped her arm through his, grateful for his steady presence as they moved through the crowd again. But as the night wore on, she couldn't quite shake the way Thomas's words lingered in her mind.

"Because you said you loved him."

The memory of his voice, his unguarded honesty, replayed in her head. It made her wonder if Thomas had been holding back more than she realized all these years.

And maybe that thought played at the back of her mind for the rest of the evening. Her sudden hyperawareness of Thomas, coupled with his revealing statement, became the catalyst for what happened when he dropped her home after the event.

She turned to him as she unbuckled her seatbelt. "Thank you, Thomas, for a lovely evening. You are always looking out for me. You are truly my best friend."

His gaze held hers, steady and unreadable. "Who wants to be more."

Kendrea inhaled sharply, her fingers stilling against the strap of her bag.

"I have always wanted to be more," Thomas continued,

his voice quieter but no less firm. "You know it. And I'm tired of being just your friend."

Kendrea closed her eyes, drawing in a shaky breath. When she opened them, Thomas had moved closer.

And then he kissed her.

His lips were warm and firm against hers, catching her completely off guard. For a moment, she froze, her mind racing to make sense of what was happening.

But then—almost as if some deep, hidden part of her finally broke free—she found herself responding. Her hands instinctively reached up to rest on his chest, feeling the rapid beat of his heart beneath her palms. The kiss was slow, deliberate, filled with a mixture of longing and certainty that left no room for doubt.

When they finally broke apart, both of them were breathing heavily, the air between them charged with an electricity she couldn't ignore.

"Thomas," Kendrea whispered, her voice trembling. "What are we doing?"

"Something we should have done long ago," Thomas said, his forehead resting lightly against hers. His eyes searched hers, filled with an intensity that made her heart ache. "I'm done pretending, Kendrea. I love you. I've loved you for as long as I can remember. And I can't keep hiding it anymore."

Her breath hitched. She wanted to say something—anything—but the emotions swirling inside her were too overwhelming.

"This was... totally unexpected," she said shakily, reaching for the door handle.

Thomas's voice was soft but certain. "Was it really?"

Kendrea hesitated for half a second before pushing the door open. "Uh... we'll address this at another time." Her voice wavered as she stepped out, her legs feeling oddly unsteady.

Thomas didn't stop her. He didn't need to.

Because they both knew—there was no going back now.

****

The phone rang, jolting Kendrea out of her journey back to that night. She reached for it hurriedly, digging it out of her bag.

"Are you home yet?" her mother's voice came over the line.

"Yes," Kendrea said groggily. "What time is it?"

"After nine," Grace Carter Sterling replied. "I haven't spoken to you in days, and before you protest—a text is not a real conversation."

Kendrea chuckled, stretching. "I hear you, Mom. How are you and George?"

"We're good—quite fine, actually. We reaped a bunch of vegetables from the farm, and I was wondering where to take yours." There was a brief pause before her mother added, "I heard on the family grapevine that you're moving in with Thomas. Why didn't you tell me?"

Kendrea blinked. "It must have slipped my mind. I thought I told you."

"No, you didn't," Grace said. "I assumed you two would get married first before taking that step."

Kendrea chuckled as she headed to the bathroom, putting her mother on speaker. "I'm not moving in with Thomas as a couple. I'm just making sure his health and fitness coach isn't taking him for granted."

"Oh," Grace said, amusement in her tone. "That's a novel

excuse for Thomas to have you living with him. That stepson of mine is quite crafty."

"Technically, we'll just be housemates."

Grace snorted. "Back in my day, if a man loved you and you loved him, you declared your feelings and moved forward. These elaborate games you people play are quite entertaining."

"Who says I love Thomas?" Kendrea asked.

"You don't have to say it," Grace replied. "He's your longest-lasting relationship with the opposite sex. You're protective of him; you'd go to war for him. When you were in high school, if I had a dollar for every time you came home fuming on Thomas' behalf, I'd be a rich woman. I've told you before, none of your other relationships have worked because you have Thomas firmly set in your mind."

"I do not," Kendrea laughed. "Mom, where are you getting these ideas from?"

Grace chuckled softly, the sound warm and knowing. "Oh, Kendrea, you can fool yourself, but you can't fool me. Mothers see these things, darling. You've been orbiting each other for years, and one day, you'll realize it's not just out of habit."

Kendrea rolled her eyes, even though her mother couldn't see her. "Mom, we're friends—really good friends. That's all it is. I care about him, sure, but that doesn't mean we're destined for some epic romance."

"Hmm," Grace hummed, clearly unconvinced. "I'll call him to pick up the vegetables—he usually swings by on Thursdays. Will you be seeing him tomorrow?"

"I will, actually. We're meeting at his house to check the progress. It's not exactly move-in ready yet."

"Good," her mother said with a chuckle. "I'll send your portion of the veggies, and please don't let them spoil. I know you don't cook if you can help it."

"I won't, Mom," Kendrea promised, stepping into the bathroom and turning on the shower.

"How's the engagement party planning going?" Grace asked.

"It's going," Kendrea groaned. "This party keeps getting bigger and bigger.

Grace chuckled. "I don't mind. Kenny is my only child who is doing something big. Both Kenice and Kenesha had small, intimate weddings. Kenneth Junior got married overseas and only remembered to tell us three months later. And honestly, I expect you'll do the same—wake up one morning, do it, and then send me a text after."

Kendrea laughed. "You know me so well."

"I do," Grace said. "And that's why I think you should get serious about Thomas already. Don't wait until someone snatches him."

"Noted," Kendrea murmured.

"But will it be heeded?" Grace asked playfully before saying goodbye.

Kendrea hung up with a small smile, shaking her head at her mother's persistence. Grace had always been good at planting seeds—subtle (or not-so-subtle) hints that took root no matter how much Kendrea resisted.

She stepped into the warm shower spray, letting the water wash over her as she tried to shake the lingering effects of the conversation.

Her mother made it sound so simple, so inevitable. But life was more complicated than that.

Wasn't it?

As the water cascaded over her, she found herself thinking about the upcoming engagement party. Thomas would be there, of course. He was always there—always had been, showing up in a way no one else ever did.

Her constant, her confidant, her everything.

The realization hit her with a force that made her grip the edge of the shower wall for support. She closed her eyes, her heart pounding in a way that had nothing to do with the hot water.

Could her mother be right? Was she fooling herself by dismissing the possibility of having something more with Thomas?

She thought about how he looked at her when he didn't think she noticed, how his touch lingered just a little longer than necessary, and how he always seemed to know what she needed even before she did.

By the time she stepped out of the shower, her mind was racing with questions she wasn't sure she wanted answers to.

She dried off, changed into her pajamas, and stood before the painting she wanted to create for his living room, hoping to distract herself with it. But even as she tried to focus, her thoughts kept drifting back to Thomas and the conversation with her mother.

Her phone buzzed, pulling her attention to the screen.

It was Thomas. He always texted her before he went to bed.

I'm going to bed early. I had a hell of a night last night, but today, I was temperate with my eating, so there was no heartburn. I'm really looking forward to the next six months—not only because I'll be losing weight, but also because I'll be staying in the same place as you.

Kendrea stared at the message, her fingers hovering over the keyboard as a small smile played on her lips.

Aww, she texted back. That's sweet. But I'm a bore to live with.

Just seeing you in the space will be a new adventure for me. Goodnight.

She hit send and set the phone down, but the warmth in her chest lingered.

Maybe it was time to stop hiding from her feelings for Thomas.

Chapter Nine

The Ridgeview house was a four-bedroom, four-bath home with a two-bedroom guesthouse. The guesthouse was some distance from the main house, situated in the back garden with its own private area. Kendrea was going to put Amanda and Stephanie in the guest house. The guest house was far enough away from the main house but close enough that Amanda didn't have far to walk to work. If Amanda thought she would be in the main house seducing Thomas, she had a little surprise coming. Kendrea had furnished the guest house first; it was move-in ready. She had even put utensils, plates, pots, and pans in the kitchenette.

It had a cozy beach house feel, and she had played on that theme. The walls were painted a soft seafoam green, and the furniture featured light, natural wood finishes that complemented the airy space. She'd added navy blue and sandy beige pops through the throw pillows, area rugs, and curtains. On the walls, she had hung framed artwork of serene beachscapes, which were really good; she had gotten them from a local artist at a fraction of the price they were worth.

The living area had a comfortable sectional sofa and a sleek coffee table that was perfect for unwinding after work. A small dining nook with a round table and four chairs sat close to the kitchenette, which was outfitted with modern appliances and everything Amanda and Stephanie could possibly need. She had even stocked the pantry with a few essentials—tea, coffee, sugar, and some basic spices—so they could settle in without any hassle.

The bedrooms were equally inviting. Kendrea had chosen crisp white bedding accented with ocean-inspired throws and cushions. Each room had a large window that let in plenty of natural light. She had even outfitted the bathrooms with fluffy towels and high-end toiletries.

She stood back and admired her work. The guest house had every comfort, and it was perfect—she would have stayed there if she hadn't wanted to send a clear message to Amanda that she had her own space. Any plans Amanda might have had to ingratiate herself to Thomas by hovering around the main house would have been thwarted.

Kendrea's phone buzzed, pulling her out of her thoughts. It was Thomas.

"Where are you?"

"In the guest house," Kendrea said. "Are you here already?"

"Yes," Thomas said. "It all looks good, and it's move-in ready. What are we waiting for?"

"Wait, stop!" Kendrea gasped. "Don't walk through without me. Have you been upstairs?"

"No," Thomas snorted. "I'm sitting in the living room. I got tired just walking from the front to where I am now, in the kitchen. I have food."

Kendrea groaned. "Do you want to come over to the guest house?"

"Nope. Take pictures," Thomas said.

"You are really not coming to tour your own guest house?" Kendrea asked shrilly.

"Have pity on me, Kendrea. I'm a hungry man. I haven't eaten since eleven o'clock. It's five o'clock now. Come join me."

"What type of food is it?"

"Homemade. Your mom made it. She said it was for us. I smell curry goat."

"Say no more," Kendrea hung up the phone, locked up the guest house, and walked briskly to the main house's back entrance. The brick pathway was lined on both sides with blooming plants. There were security cameras tucked along the way. She used her swipe card to open the back door. She entered a mudroom and laundry area that she had already outfitted with washing machines and dryers. It could use some more personal touches. She did staging work for Richard Tinsdale, and this looked like one of the staged houses she usually did. All of the downstairs had that professionally staged look. She hadn't even removed the plastic from some of the furniture.

The first floor had the gym, housekeeper's quarters, a large living room, a formal dining room, a spacious kitchen, and a cozy family room tucked off to the side. Kendrea noticed that everything was spotless but lacked the lived-in warmth she wanted the home to have. The neutral color palette, while sophisticated, felt a little too impersonal. She made a mental note to add some personal touches—maybe some colorful throw pillows, family photos, and a few statement pieces to give the space more character.

When she stepped into the kitchen, the aroma of curry goat hit her, making her stomach growl. Thomas was seated at the large island, already helping himself to a heaping plate of food. He looked up when she entered and grinned.

"There she is," he said, waving her over. "I thought you might let me starve to death."

Kendrea rolled her eyes but couldn't help smiling. "You? Starve? Not a chance."

She grabbed a plate and began serving herself. Her mom's cooking was legendary, and the spread didn't disappoint—curry goat, rice and peas, fried plantains, and a fresh green salad.

Thomas watched her as she joined him at the island. "Down here looks incredible. I feel like I'm in a fancy hotel with a fabulous view."

"Thanks, but I want it to feel like a home, not just an impersonal place to stay. I have some finishing touches coming."

"Well, I like it," he said, digging into his food. "You've got an eye for detail, and when I've eaten and the food settles down a bit, I'll go upstairs to see what you did."

"Only one bedroom is furnished," Kendrea said. "It's not yet showpiece-worthy, but you can see the look I'm going for."

"And I'll love it," Thomas smiled.

Her eyes lingered on his lips. What in heaven's name was going on with her? This felt like the Chamber of Commerce dinner all over again, the heightened awareness of Thomas. She dragged her eyes back to his, and he grinned wider.

"When you get that sultry look in your eye, what's that about?" Thomas asked.

"I'm short-circuiting, my wires are crossed," Kendrea cleared her throat.

"For how long have your wires been crossed?" Thomas asked.

"Since the Chamber of Commerce dinner," Kendrea said. "Why the hell did you kiss me?"

"Because I wanted to. I've wanted to since I was fifteen, and I just went for it," Thomas said. "I expected you to slap me or something, not melt in my arms, and then afterward pretend like it never happened."

"I'm not pretending that it didn't happen," Kendrea sighed. "I don't want to break our friendship."

"We don't have to break our friendship," Thomas said. "We can enhance it."

"If we break up," Kendrea said, "there's no way we can avoid each other. Our parents are married, and we have regular family get-togethers. I hope to get a shop at Yasmin's building, which means I would work quite close to you. If we pursue something deeper, it would be risky. If we meet up again, it would be awkward."

"I don't know," Thomas shrugged. "You seemed pretty fine when you ran into your ex, Dean Gardener."

Kendrea sighed. "Why, out of all the guys I've dated, are you so jealous of Dean?"

"He is your most significant ex. You slept with him," Thomas said. "He was your first and longest relationship, you loved him deeply. For all I know, you still love him."

"I do not," Kendrea sputtered. "I shouldn't have told you about me and Dean. You are so hypocritical. I don't go off the deep end when you have a girlfriend."

"You may not go off into a jealous rage, but you do get jealous and hypercritical," Thomas said. "Name one of the girls I've ever dated that you've liked."

"Because they're all skanks and users," Kendrea frowned.

"Not Tracy Weatherspoon," Thomas mused. "She

actually genuinely liked me. And you hated her totally and completely. You couldn't call her a gold digger either—her family is rich."

"She called you Sir Fatty," Kendrea said.

"It was a joke between us," Thomas smiled. "Maybe we would have worked if she hadn't gone to Japan for two years."

"Why are we talking about exes again?" Kendrea huffed.

"Because you said we couldn't be more than friends because of a million reasons, then you assumed we would break up and wouldn't be able to be cordial to each other," Thomas pointed out easily. "And I pointed out that you were friendly with Dean Gardener, a man you were with for close to two years when you met up at a function."

"Do you know why Dean and I broke up?" Kendrea asked.

"You said something about not being on the same page," Thomas shrugged. "To tell you the truth, I was so happy that you broke things off with him that I think I may have missed the specific reason."

"I didn't give you a specific reason," Kendrea said. "But the reason had to do with the fact that he wanted to get married, and I did not. At least not when I was just twenty-one. The women in my family tend to get married early, but I did not want that for myself. And so I told him, 'Let's wait a couple more years and see where things lead,' and he said he was fine with it. But he wasn't, not really. He started to really harass me about it. I felt pressured. I don't like feeling pressured."

Thomas nodded. "I know."

"And so I called it quits, and he moved to Kingston," Kendrea started eating. "There was no major blow-up, no cheating—just me not wanting to be tied down at the time."

"So what about now?" Thomas asked. "How do you feel

about marriage?"

"Neutral," Kendrea shrugged. "Things are finally picking up for me business-wise. I'm in a good headspace. I don't know about the future. I haven't dated in forever, but I do get lonely. Maybe that's why I'm reacting the way I am with you."

Thomas laughed. "I'll take it. I'm not picky at all. If you're sexually frustrated, I'll gladly help you with that too."

"Wait a minute," Kendrea frowned. "I'm not going there. I can't deny that I have thought about it. More times recently than I should, but all good things end."

"And if it ends," Thomas said, "I think the thing that would happen most with us is that we would tiptoe around each other for a while and then go back to being friends."

"Oh yeah?" Kendrea raised an eyebrow.

"I never want you out of my life," Thomas shrugged. "Once I'm alive, I'll be there for you. I think you and I were meant to traverse this life together, even if we are not romantically involved. So whether we are friends, stepbrother, and sister, or work across from each other, there's an unbreakable bond between us that will never go away. And I think you know that." Thomas looked at her knowingly.

Kendrea looked away, her heart pounding. Thomas had always been a constant in her life, a safe harbor in the storm, but now he was offering her something deeper that terrified her. She fiddled with her fork, the food on her plate forgotten.

"I don't think I would be so casual towards you. Therefore, I don't want to change anything."

He leaned forward, resting his elbows on the counter, his gaze steady and unflinching. "Everything's already changed, Kendrea. You feel it too—I know you do. Why fight it?"

She shook her head. "A sexual relationship is a big step,

and it's not something I take lightly."

Thomas reached for her hand. It sent shivers along her nerves and made her feel unsteady like the ground beneath her had shifted. His touch was warm, steady, and comforting, yet it ignited a spark she hadn't anticipated. Kendrea's breath caught in her throat as she stared down at his hand over hers, her mind waging war against her heart.

"Kendrea," he said softly, his voice like a soothing balm. "I'm not asking you to take this lightly. I'm asking you to trust me. To trust us. We've always had something... different, something that's more than just friendship. We owe it to ourselves to see what this can become."

Her lips parted, but no words came out. How could she explain the fear twisting in her chest? The fear of losing him, of taking a leap and falling flat. "And if it doesn't work?" she asked finally, her voice barely above a whisper. "If we ruin everything?"

Thomas's thumb traced a gentle circle on her hand, and she felt the weight of his gaze on her. "If it doesn't work, we'll figure it out. Like we always do. But Kendrea... what if it does? What if we've been standing in our own way this whole time?"

Her chest tightened as his words sank in. He was right— she did feel it too. This pull between them had grown stronger every passing year, and she had just ignored it.

"I don't know if this is great timing," she admitted. "You need to concentrate on losing weight and sorting out your feelings for Amanda."

"There are no feelings for Amanda to sort out," Thomas' hands tightened on hers. "And I can do two things at once— lose weight and still have a relationship with you. Stop overthinking this. You'll be here for six months, and maybe you won't want to leave when that time is up."

"We'll see how things play out," she said slowly.

Thomas's face lit up with a smile that made her heart ache in the best way. "I have never felt so excited about anything as I am about the upcoming months. I have a feeling this is the beginning of something extraordinary."

Chapter Ten

Two weeks later, Kendrea was running around her room, frantically packing her bags to move into the Ridgeview house. Thomas, Amanda, and Stephanie had already moved in. She was the last one to move, but she had a good reason: the engagement party was tomorrow night, and she had a few loose ends to tie up. Packing had been the last thing on her mind.

Her sisters Kenice and Kenisha had already arrived with their husbands. They were staying at the family house with their mom and George, but they had come early to help with the decorations and to help her move.

"Bless their hearts," Kendrea looked at them fondly. They all looked alike—the Carter girls, to some extent or another. They all had the classic doll face, smooth brown skin, and deep-set eyes that made them unmistakably their mother's daughters. Their hair was styled differently: Kenice wore hers short, Kenisha had long braids, and Kendrea had her curls straightened.

Her sisters were helpful women, but they were also quite nosy. And at the moment, she was getting a million and one questions from both of them regarding her current situation with Thomas.

Kenisha, especially, was rabidly curious. "So you two kissed a couple of months ago?"

"Yes," Kendrea murmured, throwing a handful of blouses into the suitcase.

"Like tongues entangled and all of that?" Kenisha asked.

"Yep," Kendrea said patiently.

"Oh, wow," Kenisha whistled. "So, how did that make you feel?"

"Like I wanted to jump him, drag off his clothes, and ride him like a horse," Kendrea said. "Is that what you want to hear, Miss Counselor?" Kenisha was a school counselor who was doing her master's, and no doubt she was practicing her counseling tactics on her.

Kenisha laughed, throwing back her head and clutching her belly.

Kenice joined her.

"I would have gone for it. Big needy guys make the best lovers," Kenice said when she sobered up. "You do know Dave and I had sex on the first date."

"No," Kenisha widened her eyes, shifting her attention from Kendrea. "Not straitlaced church man, Dave."

Kendrea smiled. Thanks to Kenice, she had a respite.

Kenice always had some sexual adventurous tales to tell. She was unapologetically uninhibited. After graduating high school, she left home and worked as a masseuse at a massage parlor in Kingston, where they offered additional services to specific clients.

Their mother had called it what it was—prostitution—

but Kenice had not cared for that label. She had moved on from that after a year and, at one point, was living with a man who already had two "wives." It was a shock to them all when, four years ago, Kenice announced that she was getting married for real to a guy she loved and couldn't see her life without him.

"How did you know you couldn't live without Dave?" Kendrea interrupted Kenice and Kenisha.

"I just knew," Kenice said. "It's like a quiet certainty. I knew him for a while; he used to come to my store and browse around and chit-chat with me, and I got this vibe that he was the one. So when he asked me on a date, I said yes. And the rest, they say, is history."

Kendrea nodded and turned to Kenisha. "How did you know Nigel was the one?"

"I had a giant crush on the guy," Kenisha said. "You all know this. He taught at the same school—he was fine. I was not the only one drooling over him, so I was excited when the principal asked him to consult me on a disciplinary issue involving one of his students. I acted like a nervous ninny. Anyway, it so happens that he liked me too. Like led to love, and I was a virgin on my wedding night. I will happily say."

"Virginity is overrated," Kenice snorted. "Virginity does not guarantee a happy marriage."

"I know that," Kenisha snorted. "You get defensive whenever I mention virginity because you've had more partners than Kendrea has shoes."

"Oh, here we go again," Kendrea rolled her eyes.

"What's going on?" Kenny asked from the door. She had entered the house without them hearing.

Kendrea grinned. "Big sister! What's going on is that Kenisha is slut-shaming Kenice, and she is about to puritan-shame Kenisha. But now that you're here, we can move on to other topics, like your engagement party."

Kenny chuckled. "So, just a regular day in the Carter girls' life, huh?"

"That's quite right," Kendrea nodded.

Both Kenice and Kenisha got up to greet Kenny vociferously. The discussion turned to food; they ordered takeout, and Kendrea finished packing.

"So, who is going to stay here when Kendrea leaves?" Kenisha asked Kenny. "This place would be a nice income earner."

"My friend Tiffany will stay here in the other room and pay the utility bills," Kendrea said. "Kenny is not ready to rent out her place yet."

"Yep," Kenny nodded. "I have a special attachment to this place. Besides, Kendrea will need a place to stay after her six months with Thomas are up."

Kenice snorted. "Kendrea's not coming back here. I told you the same thing when you move in with Camden."

"True," Kenny nodded. "You did prophesy something like that."

"And I was right," Kenice grinned.

"I could stay in the guest cottage after Amanda and Stephanie leave," Kendrea mused. "It's cozy and pretty. I did a great job with it if I should say so myself."

"Stop fronting. You'll be in Thomas' room," Kenice said. "I wish I lived in Montego Bay again. I would have so many living options. Thomas' old apartment, Kenny's place, Thomas and Kendrea's guest house."

Kendrea smiled. She liked how Kenice paired her with Thomas.

"So, why don't you move?" Kenny asked. "Open another branch of your store here in Montego Bay? We can always do with another health food store."

"I can't," Kenice groaned. "Dave just got promoted at his bank. It's a great career opportunity."

"It would have been nice to have you living close," Kendrea grinned. "You are the most lively of the four of us."

"That I am," Kenice said. "Kenny is boring, Kenisha is a prude, you and I could have some fun."

Kenisha glared at them. "I am not a prude. I have values and standards. After Mommy had Kenneth Junior, Kenny, and myself, the moral integrity of our lineage slipped dangerously with you and corrected itself somewhat with Kendrea."

Kendrea and Kenny laughed.

"Please don't take on Kenisha," Kenny pleaded with Kenice. "You know people who know you casually would be shocked to know how childish the two of you can act when you are together."

"But Kenny, I need to address Miss Prude's assertions that I, Kenice Carter Wilson, am somehow inferior to her."

"Another time," Kenny said. "Did I tell you that DJ Duke will be performing at my engagement dinner?"

"What?" Kenisha and Kenice asked at the same time.

It was enough to shift the conversation. It would be peaceful for a while.

Kendrea got up. "I knew already, of course. I'm just going to grab a couple of things I forgot while you guys talk about it."

****

They arrived at the Byfields' mansion a little after eight on Saturday morning to decorate the engagement area.

"Now, this is how I want to live," Kenice whistled when they got out of the car. "The garden is stunning. I wonder if

Lorraine Byfield wants to give us a tour of the inside?"

"It's equally as stunning," Kendrea murmured. "She changes the décor every year. She is, after all, an interior designer."

"How was she as a boss?" Kenisha asked.

"Great," Kendrea said. "She rarely came into the office. Hers is a large outfit with multiple teams handling different aspects of design and project management. She trusted us to handle the day-to-day operations, but she had an incredible eye for detail when she did show up. She always had this calm, confident energy, like she knew exactly what she wanted."

Kenice raised an eyebrow. "So why did you leave? Sounds like a dream job."

"It was, in many ways," Kendrea admitted as they walked toward the sprawling garden. The towering fountain at the center caught the sunlight, sending rainbows glistening across the flower beds. "But it wasn't my dream. I wanted to do my own thing, build something of my own. Lorraine was supportive when I told her I was leaving—she even referred me to my first few clients."

"Wow, that's classy of her," Kenice said, clearly impressed. "Not everyone is like that in business."

Kendrea nodded. "She's a class act, no doubt about it. But make no mistake, she's also a perfectionist. If something isn't right, she'll point it out, no matter how small. It's one of the reasons this place looks like it belongs in a magazine."

"I am surprised she's allowing you to decorate her backyard for her son's engagement party," Kenisha whispered as they approached the door.

"I'm not decorating the whole backyard," Kendrea whispered. "Back there is about three acres; we're just doing the tables. She had her events team do all the setup already—we're just going to add the finishing touches: centerpieces, table runners, and some accent lighting. It's ten tables. Her team, I assume, will be doing the rest."

Kendrea pressed the doorbell at the imposing front door, and Lorraine herself answered.

She looked at them, blinking. "Oh my goodness, what a stunning group of women."

Kendrea grinned. "Thanks, Lorraine. These are my sisters, Kenice and Kenisha."

"Ah yes, lovely to meet you," Lorraine hugged them in turn. "I know Kenny had other sisters besides Kendrea; I didn't know you were all so pretty. Come on in. We'll head straight to the back where a bevy of activity is going on."

"So, what is the age ranking between you all again?" Lorraine asked.

"We are two years apart," Kendrea answered. Kenneth Junior is the oldest and only boy; he's thirty-two. Kenny is the oldest girl, soon to be thirty. Then there's Kenisha, Kenice, and then me."

"I love it," Lorraine chuckled. "Your parents had it all planned out perfectly."

"Actually, my mom said it wasn't planned," Kendrea answered. Kenice and Kenisha were too busy looking around at the interior décor to be polite. Kenice's mouth was halfway open.

Lorraine, seeing their fascination, chuckled. "I'll give you ladies a tour at another time. After all, you'll soon be family; we should be better acquainted. We'll have lunch in the future."

"I would love that," Kenice finally said.

They headed toward the patio doors, which opened to the breathtaking view. Immediately before them were lush, terraced lawns, and beyond that, the beautiful Caribbean

Sea and the Jamaican coastline.

"Watch your step," Lorraine said as she walked across the terrace and beside an infinity pool. "We have odds and ends scattered around. I decided to match my Christmas décor this year to Kenny and Camden's burgundy and silver theme so that there's a seamless transition."

They walked down to another large terrace area that was being transformed. Indeed, there was a buzz of activity taking place. The expansive terrace, perfectly paved with polished stone, had the same breathtaking view as above.

The area was partially shaded by elegantly draped canopies, their soft white fabric swaying lightly in the ocean breeze. People were setting up twinkling string lights above the fabric.

Large floral arrangements in burgundy and silver hues were already stationed at key points, each featuring roses, dahlias, and eucalyptus, with a touch of baby's breath for softness. The tables Kendrea was to work with were arranged in a semi-circle, covered in crisp white linen with burgundy runners that shimmered subtly in the daylight. The chairs were dressed in matching burgundy and silver covers, tied with satin bows.

A dance floor took center stage, bordered by additional string lights and flanked by tall arrangements in ornate silver stands. On one side, a small stage was set up for speeches or possibly a live band, and equipment was already in place.

Nearby, a buffet table was being arranged, complete with silver chafing dishes and intricate platters waiting to be filled. There was also a bar area, its counters lined with sparkling glassware.

Beyond the terrace, a gently sloping path led to a lawn. A few additional seating areas were set up with plush lounge furniture, perfect for guests wanting a quieter moment amidst the festivities.

Different groups of people kept trickling in and out of the area.

"This is spectacular," Kenice whispered, wide-eyed, as she took it all in.

"I feel like I'm on the set of a luxury wedding magazine shoot," Kenisha added, her voice full of awe.

Kendrea nodded in agreement. "It's definitely one of the most elegant setups I've worked on. Let's make sure our pieces elevate it even more."

Lorraine nodded. "I trust your vision. The side gate is open for you to bring your things around. I'll leave you to it. If you need anything, I'll be inside checking on the catering team."

Chapter Eleven

Thomas thought he would have a hard time finding something to wear to the engagement party. He had a few semi-formal clothes, or what he considered to be semi-formal, all but one pair of pants could be buttoned around his waist. Or so he thought until he started trying them on and found that they were not as tight as before. All but one of them actually fit him comfortably.

It had been a week since he started the weight loss program with Amanda. One week.

Amanda had warned him that they would ease into a routine and that he should curb his expectations. He hadn't expected to lose weight, but it seemed as if he had. He spun around in the mirror like an excited boy. It was probably only water weight, but he felt good. He didn't feel deprived or hungry. Stephanie had cooked some tasty meals so far. She went heavy on the vegetables, but he didn't mind, and the only exercise Amanda had him doing was walking on the beach.

They had discovered that the private cove at Ridgeview was two miles long. She had him do a lap every day in the evenings because that was his most comfortable exercise time. After walking with him the first evening, she sat and watched him on the bluff as he did it.

"A coach doesn't need to exercise too," she had grinned at him, "just to ensure that you do it. I prefer getting my steps in the morning. You can join me if you want. I could make sure you go a little harder."

"Interesting," he had responded. "I think I can go harder."

"That's great," Amanda had grinned. "I will send you your schedule for next week this evening. We're going to throw in some weights. Beginner stuff. Nothing to worry about."

And so it had begun. Thomas rubbed some light gel in his hair, slapped some aftershave on his face, and stared at himself in the mirror. Even his face looked a little leaner—or maybe he was imagining things. He would wait to hear what Kendrea had to say. He couldn't wait until she moved in with him.

He met up with Amanda in the driveway while walking out. She was just about to get into her car. She stopped and whistled at him flirtatiously.

"You clean up well, Mr. Sterling."

He grinned. "I was just thinking that a week has done me good and boosted my confidence. You, my dear, are going to be worth every penny."

Amanda chortled with laughter. "So, where are you off to?"

"My stepsister's engagement party," Thomas said. "I told you I was going a couple of days ago."

"Oh, it was tonight?" Amanda widened her eyes. "Where's your date?"

"I don't have one," Thomas said. "I'm flying solo tonight. Where are you off to?"

"A family function," Amanda said, "but it was canceled, so I was just going to go to Mingles to see what that's about."

"Ah, I heard it was a hot spot," Thomas nodded. "I've never been myself, but I'm sure this is too early."

"They have a restaurant," Amanda said. "I don't mind taking myself out now and again. Maybe I'll find someone who might be in the same predicament."

"True," Thomas nodded. "You never know who you'll meet. Enjoy yourself, Amanda."

He waved to her and got into his vehicle. As he drove off, he briefly wondered if she had expected him to invite her to the party as his plus one. He almost went back to ask her if she wanted to come but changed his mind. He wanted to spend as much time with Kendrea as he could tonight.

He pulled up to the Byfields' mansion. They had started decorating for Christmas, so the palm trees that lined their generous driveway were strung with lights. He was directed to park, by men in vests, in a spot close to the house. It seemed as if he was early. He breathed a sigh of relief—he hadn't been exercising that long to be parking far and then walking to the venue without being out of breath or breaking a sweat.

When he arrived, the live band was just tuning up. His sister Yasmin greeted him at the entrance to the side gate with a hug. She was dressed in a little burgundy dress and had a silver usher pin on her dress.

"Thomas!" she hugged him. "You look fantastic. Why's that?"

Thomas laughed. "You haven't seen me in three weeks. I'm cleanly shaved. It could be that."

"Nah," Yasmin shook her head. "You seem taller."

"Last I checked, I was still six feet tall," Thomas shrugged. "Am I too early?"

"No," Yasmin said. "Family got a different time because of pictures. Dad and Grace aren't here yet, but everyone else is."

"I see," he chuckled.

"The photographer is taking random shots at the poolside now. I'll join you guys in a moment."

Kendrea was posing with her sisters when he walked to the poolside. They all looked gorgeous, but his eyes focused on Kendrea.

In a room full of beautiful women, she would always be the most beautiful to him . She radiated it, and it always drew him in like a moth to a flame.

"Hey," Camden said behind him.

"Hey man, congrats again." Thomas grinned. "We have another label to add to our association—brother-in-law."

Camden nodded. "As well as neighbor. I heard you moved in next door."

"That I did," Thomas nodded.

"No doubt we'll see each other regularly. I hear Kenny is planning to have Sunday brunches with Kendrea and Audra living close by. You, me, and Jairo can no doubt watch football together. I turned my guest house into a man cave."

Thomas laughed. "I have my health and fitness coach and chef living in mine."

"I'm proud of you for doing something about your health." Camden clapped him on the back. "By the way, did you get an email from Alan?"

"I haven't checked," Thomas frowned.

"It should be in your inbox," Camden said. "In essence, he apologizes for sending you the previous mail. After speaking with the partners at his firm, he's unable to represent Nicole

Pink."

"Good, thanks," Thomas nodded. "How badly did you lambast him?"

"Bad." Camden grinned. "Nobody else would take such a frivolous case, which they would be guaranteed to lose, besides the conflict of interest. She has him sprung."

"So, I guess she'll be here tonight then?" Thomas frowned. "As Alan's date?"

Camden laughed. "Nope. Kendrea called me and told me to tell Alan that Nicole was not welcome as a plus one to any family events where the Sterlings and Carters were an integral part of. I told Alan. He didn't even bat an eyelid—he said he would take someone else. Apparently, the man has dates on standby. Nicole is not the only option on his menu."

"Kendrea did that?" Thomas whispered.

"Yup," Camden said. "Kendrea will go to war when it comes to you. I've genuinely never met a woman more fiercely protective of someone who's not her man like Kendrea is of you."

"Is that so?" Thomas grinned. He felt happy hearing that, almost like floating off the balcony.

"If you can't make the moving-in stunt you're pulling with her work, then I will be severely disappointed in you," Camden said.

"How did you know it's a stunt?" Thomas asked. "Is it that obvious?"

"Yup," Camden nodded. "I think even she knows it's a stunt and is going along with it to see how the two of you would work. Don't make the same mistake I did with Kenny, letting her wait long before I popped the question. You and I both know that Kendrea Carter is a keeper. Don't mess it up."

****

He could barely get any alone time with Kendrea at the party. They were both in great demand by members of their various families. His grand aunt Florence pulled him aside and wouldn't let him go for a good while. She wanted to talk about her will, of all things.

Every time he made to leave, she squinted at him. "I'm leaving a million dollars to you, Thomas. The least you could do is hang out with your old aunty for a little."

Thomas chuckled. "Aunt Florence, I don't need to be bribed to have a conversation with you. I just want to go and find Kendrea."

"I like Kendrea," Florence nodded. "She's a good one. I heard about that other one, Nicole. She likened you to a pig and then a cow? You dodged a bullet with that one."

"Did Abby tell everybody about the conversation?" Thomas frowned.

"I doubt it," Florence snorted. "She lives with me—my only grandchild that I can tolerate for a long period of time. We gossip about the family. Forgive her for sharing. I was so angry on your behalf that I had to take something to calm my nerves."

"Thank you," Thomas kissed his aunt on her forehead, "but I don't want you popping pills on my behalf."

Florence cackled. "They were herbal pills."

"Marijuana?" Thomas raised his eyebrows. "How many times should I tell you to stay away from drugs?"

Florence laughed even louder. "They were doctor-prescribed, not marijuana. You are not taking drugs, are you, Thomas?"

"Never have," Thomas said. "Though one time, a friend

of mine almost got me to lose weight by smoking. He said it worked to keep him slim."

"Thank God you didn't do that," Florence replied. "Your grand uncle struggled to quit smoking. I told him he had to do it when we had our first child together because secondhand smoke was no joke. Can you believe it? He quit, but thirty years later, he died from lung cancer anyway."

Thomas inhaled. He loved his grand aunt, he really did, but now came the Rupert segment of her reminiscing—and this could take a while. He settled into his seat with resignation on his face when Kendrea came up to them.

"Aunt Florence, can I borrow Thomas for a little? I want to introduce him to a neighbor."

"Oh sure, dear." Florence nodded.

"Thank you," Thomas breathed when they were out of earshot.

"I glanced over at you and knew you were due for a rescue," Kendrea chuckled. "I want you to meet Jairo Jones and his cousin, DJ Duke. I know you know of them, but you haven't officially met either of them."

They were heading toward two tall, muscular, and handsome men—the kind of men that women didn't take their eyes off when they entered a room.

He tried to pull in his belly a little but decided against it because all it was doing was making him lightheaded. He released a breath, and Kendrea looked over at him and smiled. "They have nothing on you, handsome."

Thomas grinned. "I was feeling a little intimidated by all the muscles."

"You'll get there." Kendrea tucked her arm in his. "And even if you don't, I will always love you through thick or thin, muscular or flabby."

Thomas smiled. "I wish you meant that romantically."

"We'll see," Kendrea said mysteriously.

Thomas let her words linger in the air, unsure how to respond. Kendrea had a way of dropping little comments that kept him guessing. They approached the two men, who greeted Kendrea warmly and extended firm handshakes to Thomas.

"Thomas, my neighbor, it's great to meet you," Jairo said with an easy smile, his voice deep and commanding. "Kendrea has told me a lot about you."

"Good things, I hope?" Thomas replied, glancing at Kendrea, who gave him an innocent shrug.

"Mostly," Jairo said. "She said you were a staunch supporter of the LC Foster Little League club, but I can't hold that against you. My son's league is their fierce adversary."

Thomas laughed. "I do support that club. My housekeeper's grandson goes to that school, and she commanded me to be their sponsor when they were hunting around for one."

"Oh," Jairo chuckled, "well, that's all right then. It's all good. That was a generous gesture. We need more entrepreneurs like yourself to invest in the youth of this country, and I'm happy you decided to focus on football. Are you a fan?"

"Not really," Thomas said. "I'm a bit of a wagonist of all sports. Whenever something momentous is happening, I tune in. For example, when you were making waves in Europe, I suddenly became interested in the English Premier League. When you left, my interest waned."

"That's honest," Jairo said.

"And sounds just like me," Duke chuckled. "I like you already, Thomas. I see I'll enjoy living at Ridgeview with good people around."

"You're moving here?" Thomas asked.

"Yes," Duke said. "Sort of. I'll be dividing my time

between here and Kingston. I'm focusing on a few business interests on this side. I already asked Kendrea to decorate for me like she did Jairo's and your place."

"I asked Richard, and he said all the units were gone," Thomas said.

"They were," Duke smiled. "The person who was going to buy the townhouse beside Jairo's dropped out. How cool is that?"

"Way cool," Kendrea said happily. "I get to decorate your house. That will be three out of five houses at the exclusive Ridgeview. And I'm plotting to get Richard to let me decorate his place if he decides to keep it for himself."

"D.J. Duke," Yasmin said from behind them, "you'll be up shortly."

"Sure," Duke nodded. "Guys, it was a pleasure. I'm sure we'll be seeing more of each other when I move to this neck of the woods."

"Ooh," Kendrea said, "can you do my favorite song?"

"Which one is your favorite again?" Duke asked.

"It's Always You," Thomas said.

Duke nodded. "Of course, I'll leave it for the last number. Kenny already requested it. Out of all the songs I've done, this one seems to be resonating with everybody."

"Because it's everyone's wish," Kendrea said wistfully. "We all want a ride or die, someone who'll play for keeps, through thick and thin, tried and true, someone who will stick with you…"

Thomas didn't know if she was aware she had moved closer to him, but he took advantage of the situation and linked his arm through hers, silently communicating that he was her ride or die, through thick and thin.

Chapter Twelve

"**H**ow was the engagement party?" Amanda asked as they set out for their morning walk.

"It was great—beautiful. It was a large gathering, but it felt intimate." Thomas blinked at her groggily. "Do people really wake up at this hour to go torture themselves every day?"

"Yes, they do," Amanda laughed, "and they like it too."

"How was your Mingles foray?" Thomas asked after a while. He seemed lost in thought. It would have been nice if he had given her more details on the engagement party. She wanted in. She wanted to know the man—what made him tick.

"It was great," Amanda said. "Their food was good, and the company entertaining. It turns out that Mingles is the hot spot for entertainment, even though I went early. I met several guys—young professionals. I have a couple of dates lined up."

"Cool," Thomas panted.

Amanda glanced at Thomas. He sounded disinterested, which was crushing. Her plan to get him interested in her was going at a snail's pace. She was wracking her brain, trying to figure out how to get through to him, but unfortunately, Thomas was not as into her as she had originally thought.

If a guy's response to her having several dates lined up was just "cool," then this was not a man who was attracted to her in any way. She had really misread their initial meeting. Was his eagerness for her to live at his place only about him losing weight?

Stephanie would die laughing when she found out that her grand plan was dying a slow death.

"So, er, when is Kendrea coming by?"

"Today," Thomas said, excitement in his eyes. "She had to do some last-minute packing and wanted to sleep in after the party. But she'll be coming today."

Amanda smiled brittlely.

Darn Kendrea. Why was she even moving in? Didn't she have a life outside of Thomas? Their relationship was weird and truly baffling. Were they in love with each other? What was the deal?

She cleared her throat. "Kendrea is truly a pretty woman. I wonder why she's single."

Thomas' steps faltered. "You're not interested in her, are you?"

"No!" Amanda stammered. "I'm straight!"

"Oh," Thomas chuckled. "Because that would be a plot twist I wouldn't have seen coming."

"But I can recognize beauty, can't I?" Amanda said. "Which leads me to believe that she's probably really picky when it comes to men. I've been accused of that more than once."

Thomas chuckled. "I don't know if Kendrea is that picky. Some of her boyfriend choices in the past have given me real heartburn. I probably gain a good twenty pounds after she dates each one. It's a good thing there haven't been that many, or I'd be much bigger."

Amanda perked up. This was invaluable information—finally, some insight into Thomas' state of mind.

"So you're that invested in who Kendrea dates?"

He nodded. "A little bit too invested. A few years ago, she got engaged, and I went off the rails."

"Kendrea was engaged?" Amanda murmured. "Who was the lucky guy?"

"Dean Gardener," Thomas said through gritted teeth. "They met in college. He was everything I wasn't—tall, slim, handsome. I had never seen her so in love. I hated every moment of it. Not because I didn't want to see her happy—I just didn't want to see her happy with anyone else but me, I guess."

Amanda's mind was ticking over. So Thomas had feelings for Kendrea? That was expected. She was the one non-family female who had been there for him through the years—through bullying, through all of his life—and she was attractive. Why wouldn't he have developed feelings?

Kendrea obviously didn't share the same sentiments. Otherwise, why would she have had other boyfriends or even gotten engaged?

Where had she heard the name Dean Gardener before?

At Mingles. That's where.

She had been sitting alone in the lounge, fuming over the fact that her carefully laid plan to get Thomas to invite her to the engagement party had fizzled. She had found out about Kenny and Camden's engagement party from Stephanie, who had overheard them talking about it. She had also known that Thomas wasn't planning to take a date, so she had dressed up, stood in the driveway, and waited for him to come out of the house—yet the man hadn't even asked her to go with him.

And then after taking her dejected self to Mingles, a tall, dark cutie had asked if the seat in front of her was taken. He had introduced himself as Dean! Was his surname Gardener? She couldn't remember if she had heard Gardener.

What she needed to do was call his number and have a conversation. If he was Kendrea's ex, then her plan was not derailed. Not in the least. She could do something with this Dean angle.

And then Thomas would be hers—putty in her hands, derailed by Kendrea's love life but way thinner and grateful to her for getting him there.

She glanced over at him and smiled serenely. "Let's pick it up a notch, why don't we?"

"Are you serious?" Thomas panted.

"You can do it," Amanda said. "Did you read Stephanie's meal plan for the week? All balanced, yummy dishes. I'm looking forward to some of them myself."

"Tell me about you and Stephanie," Thomas said. "You resemble each other a bit, but you both have different last names."

"Oh." Amanda chuckled. "We look like our mother, who married Stephanie's dad after meeting on a cruise ship. He was a rich older guy, and my mom was part of the entertainment staff. She sang and danced."

"Oh," Thomas said, looking at her. "That's interesting and romantic."

"It wasn't really," Amanda shrugged. "She knew next to nothing about him but she did find out that he was violent shortly after that, though. However, she stuck with him and then had Stephanie. A friend of hers saw her at the hospital after she got a particularly bad beating. The friend told my grandparents and they arranged for her to flee the country with Stephanie, who was about four at the time."

"Oh wow," Thomas said.

"Then Jed came out," Amanda said, flexing her muscles. "He wanted my mom back, but she initiated divorce proceedings. The lawyer she used was my father. They had an affair. He was married at the time too."

"Interesting." Thomas nodded.

"What's interesting," Amanda chuckled, "is that my mom went back to the cruise ship when I was about three and left me and Stephanie with my father and his wife, Gem, who treated us so well and loved us so unconditionally that I used to think my mother was my aunt and Gem was my real mother."

"Did she have any children of her own?" Thomas asked.

"Yes, she did—two boys, Lionel and Craig. They both died in the car crash that killed my father. Ironically, that's the reason we stayed with Aunt Gem even after our mother returned to Jamaica. She didn't want to leave Gem all alone, and she was in a new relationship and didn't want us cramping her style. We were fine with the way things were until Aunt Gem married again. We liked the guy, but we couldn't stand his kids—four of them, all under twelve. Our once peaceful house became a den of noise and mayhem. But Aunt Gem loves that kind of thing; she has a big heart."

"Steph escaped before me. She was a U.S. citizen, so she sorted out her situation pretty easily. Me, on the other hand, I had a little bit of a hiccup, but we're sorting that out. For the time being, I'm here now, and I'm happy that I can help you."

Thomas nodded. "I'm happy that you're here now too."

****

"**R**un the plan by me again?" Stephanie asked later that day.

They were sitting in the cottage. They had just spied on Kendrea and Thomas—he was moving her in, a pep in his step, looking like a man with all his Christmases happening at once.

Stephanie was preparing to go next door to cook the evening meal, lazily leafing through her recipe book.

"The plan is simple," Amanda said. "Befriend Dean Gardener, then nudge him toward Kendrea. While she's distracted with him, I make a move on Thomas."

"Oh boy," Stephanie sighed. "Are you even sure the guy you met at Mingles was Dean Gardener?"

"Yes, I'm sure. I called his number," Amanda said. "He didn't answer, but his voicemail said, 'Hey, this is Dean Gardener.' So there—mystery solved."

"So, how are you going to nudge Dean toward Kendrea?" Stephanie asked.

"I'll establish a friendship with the guy. Haven't you been listening?" Amanda asked exasperatedly. "Then I'll casually bring up Kendrea in conversation and fan the flames of interest."

Stephanie sighed. "I don't want anything to do with this elaborate gold-digging exercise. Please don't ask me to participate."

"Why are you changing your tune now?" Amanda asked. "What has changed? You were all for me bagging a rich husband when I first suggested it."

"Because I initially thought you were joking," Stephanie said. "But these are real people. I like Thomas—he's a sweet person. He doesn't deserve all these machinations around him. It wouldn't be good for either of you if you married him. You would have literally planned, plotted, and manipulated a man into marrying you just so you could get what he has."

"And people have been doing this very thing—both men and women—for hundreds of years, ever since marriage existed!" Amanda growled. "I am not the first. Stop acting brand new."

"Okay," Stephanie said. "But I'm just saying—why don't you allow things to progress naturally?"

"Because Kendrea exists," Amanda said. "She's standing in the way of my happiness. There is no 'naturally' with her around. She must be distracted by someone else so that Thomas will be interested in me."

Stephanie closed the recipe book with a thud and exhaled sharply. "Amanda, listen to yourself. You're saying you would be willing to settle for Thomas' attention even though you know he loves Kendrea."

"I don't know that," Amanda said.

"He loves her," Stephanie said. "In the office, when he was talking about being healthy for his future wife and children, he looked directly at her and paused. That's his boo, girl. If you end up with him by some stroke of luck, you will not be his first choice. You will always be under Kendrea's shadow. Let them work out their issues and go find another guy to harass."

"No!" Amanda glared at Stephanie. "Thomas is the one. He's the best candidate."

"Forcing feelings isn't going to bring you happiness." Stephanie got up and stretched. "I know this firsthand. I've been on both sides of the coin—both the forcer and the forced. And let me tell you, one morning, you'll wake up, stare at yourself in the mirror, and you'll hate yourself.

You'll think, 'What am I doing? What have I done?'"

"I will not say that," Amanda scoffed.

"Oh, brat," Stephanie chuckled. "You'll learn."

"You had better not say a word to Thomas or Kendrea," Amanda warned.

"My lips are sealed." Stephanie made a zipping motion. "I must admit, I'm finding all of this highly entertaining."

Chapter Thirteen

"So, I live here now!" Kendrea laughed with abandon as she stared out at the view. "Somebody pinch me."

Thomas pinched her and handed her a glass of carbonated water. "Courtesy of the chef. Apparently, it's supposed to keep me full. Has a dash of lime and a stevia leaf, and it's actually good."

"Ah, yes." Kendrea took a sip. "It's sweet!"

"It's a leaf from a stevia plant. She has a couple of pots of the thing and uses it as a sweetener."

"How is her food?" Kendrea asked. "Is it good?"

"So good, I think I'll keep her when all this is over. She sends me a weekly menu and puts the calories beside everything. She asked me what my favorite foods were and made healthy versions of them."

"Really?" Kendrea raised an eyebrow. "Like what?"

"Like chicken Alfredo," Thomas said, his eyes lighting up. "She makes it with some kind of cauliflower-based sauce and zucchini noodles. Sounds weird, right? But it's actually amazing."

Kendrea nodded. "Zucchini noodles? I've heard of that. She's really going all out for you."

"She is," Thomas admitted, leaning against the counter. "She even made a low-calorie cheesecake for dessert last night. It wasn't exactly Cheesecake Factory, but it was pretty close."

Kendrea laughed. "Thomas eating cauliflower and zucchini—who would've thought I'd see the day? The Thomas I knew had a weakness for triple cheeseburgers and fries."

"Still do," Thomas said with a grin. "But Stephanie's cooking is top-notch. This whole transition to eating healthier is not as bad as I thought it would be. I've even dropped a couple of pounds already."

Kendrea gave him a once-over, her smile softening. "I can see that. You look good, Thomas. Happier. Healthier."

Thomas's face flushed slightly, and he shrugged. "Thanks. I feel better too. It's like... I don't know, like I'm finally taking control of my life."

"Well, I'm glad," Kendrea said, her tone sincere. "You deserve that. It's nice to see you putting yourself first for a change. I must admit, I was skeptical about Amanda, but she and Stephanie seem to be working out fine."

Thomas nodded. "They're great."

They stood in comfortable silence for a moment, sipping their drinks and gazing out at the view. Kendrea finally broke the quiet. "So, what's next? You've got the house, the healthy meals, the new habits... what's the next big move for Thomas?"

"The next big move depends on you," Thomas said. "But we'll take it one day at a time, as agreed. No pressure."

"No pressure," Kendrea agreed. "So, what's on the menu for this evening?"

"Today is Sunday. It's the typical Sunday dinner with a twist. Instead of fried chicken, it will be air-fried chicken. And instead of mac and cheese, it's cauliflower and cheese." Thomas chuckled, rubbing the back of his neck. "I'm not gonna lie; I was initially skeptical, but Stephanie somehow makes it taste good. She's got this knack for making healthy food feel like comfort food."

Kendrea nodded. "Air-fried chicken and cauliflower cheese? I wonder if she'll mind me taking cooking lessons."

"That's part of the package," Thomas said with a smile. "I'm quite curious about how she does her desserts. They're filling, and I no longer crave sweets. Tonight's dessert is something called avocado chocolate mousse. Apparently, it's good for you."

Kendrea wrinkled her nose playfully. "Avocado in a dessert? Now that, I have to see to believe."

Thomas laughed, his shoulders relaxing. "I know, right? But trust me, she has a way of making it work."

Kendrea smiled. "I can't wait to try it. It's been a while since we've had a proper Sunday dinner together."

"Yes, it has been," Thomas said. "I'm so happy we'll be spending loads of time in each other's company."

"Me too," Kendrea said. "I'll even wake up to exercise with you guys."

"Great," Thomas said, his face lighting up.

"It might be our only quality time together," Kendrea chuckled. "The busy season is upon us. I'm booked solid for the next couple of weeks leading up to Christmas, and then there's the wedding, and then I have a—"

Thomas stopped her mid-speech with a kiss.

Kendrea froze momentarily, her words caught in her

throat as Thomas's lips pressed softly against hers. It wasn't hurried or forceful—just warm, steady, and unexpectedly tender. When he pulled back, his eyes searched hers, filled with a mix of hope and uncertainty.

"I'm sorry," Thomas said quickly, his voice barely above a whisper. "I just... I've been wanting to do that for a long time, and I couldn't let the moment pass. Besides, I'm extremely happy that you're here."

Kendrea blinked, her heart pounding in her chest. She opened her mouth to speak, but no words came out. Instead, she stared at him, trying to process what had just happened—and the feelings it stirred in her.

"Oh, sorry. Didn't mean to intrude," Stephanie said behind them. "Dinner is ready. Where would you like me to serve it?"

"On the patio, here," Thomas said.

Stephanie nodded and turned away.

Kendrea chuckled. "I feel a teeny bit embarrassed."

"Don't be." Thomas picked up his glass and handed hers to her.

"To new beginnings." He clinked his glass to hers.

"To new beginnings," Kendrea murmured.

****

"I can't believe you live here," Tiffany said the moment she stepped through the front door.

"Been here a week, and I still can't believe it either," Kendrea chuckled. "If it weren't for the fact that I have to get up out of bed and head to work, I'd think I was on vacation."

"And how are you and Thomas?" Tiffany asked.

"Great!" Kendrea said. "We exercise together in the

mornings, and I made it to dinner three times this past week. We have a lot of laughs and chat—but we have an audience. His health coach, Amanda, is there when we exercise; sometimes, she joins us for dinner—except on weekends.

"Why does he need a health coach to live with him?" Tiffany snorted.

Kendrea shrugged, grabbing a coupl e of glasses and pouring water for both of them. "Well, he's been overweight for most of his life and wanted to do it right. I'm reluctant to even say this, but Amanda is actually really good at what she does."

Tiffany took a sip of water, raising an eyebrow. "Still sounds a little extra to me. Can't he do all that without her living in his house?"

"It's not as weird as it sounds," Kendrea said, sitting across from her. "Amanda's professional, and she keeps him on track. Plus, it's working. He's already dropped a few pounds, and you can see he's got more energy."

Tiffany leaned forward, her eyes narrowing slightly. "And you're okay with it? I mean, this Amanda person being so... present?"

Kendrea hesitated for a moment before laughing lightly. "Why wouldn't I be? She's there for him, not me. Besides, she's friendly, and we get along fine. It's not like she's moving in on him or anything."

Tiffany gave her a knowing look. "But doesn't it bother you? Her spending all that time with him? Encouraging him, massaging his ego? That's... intimate, don't you think?"

Kendrea frowned, twirling her glass between her hands. "Thomas and I are friends, Tiff. That's all. Amanda's doing her job, and it's helping him. There's no reason for me to feel bothered. Besides, he says he has no feelings for her."

"Uh-huh," Tiffany said, her tone skeptical. "So you're

saying there's absolutely no part of you that feels... territorial?"

"Territorial?" Kendrea repeated, her voice rising slightly. "He's not my property."

"No, but you care about him," Tiffany said with a small smirk. "And don't try to deny it. I know you, Kendrea. All I'm saying is, keep an eye on Amanda. She might be professional, but she's still a woman, and Thomas is still a catch—whatever his size. I can just imagine how much attention he'll get when he loses the weight. People are shallow, including me. I can't wait to see him without the extra weight."

"Oh boy, here we go again," Kendrea murmured. "My sisters keep saying the same thing. Whether Thomas is fat or slim, he'll still be Thomas."

"No, girl," Tiffany shook her head. "You'll be seeing another side to the man. When you're thinner, people treat you differently, and he'll react differently. All the women who wouldn't give him a second glance before will be falling at his feet like flies. Not even he knows how he'll react to that. Will he turn wild, sleeping with them one after another, using and discarding them for punishment? Or will he stick to his old faithful Kendrea, who's been with him through thick and thin?"

"You are so fanciful," Kendrea said, eyeing her friend. "Thomas has no problem getting girls now. He's not going to turn wild."

"There's a difference between having to work for their affection and having them fawning over you like lovesick puppies," Tiffany said. "I know what I'm talking about. There was this guy at my old high school, Paul. He was a late bloomer—nobody used to pay him any attention. Then, in our final year, he developed into a gorgeous specimen of manhood. Let me tell you, even I was in the mix trying to get his attention."

Kendrea chuckled. "Did he turn into a man-whore?"

"Yes, he did," Tiffany nodded. "Slept with half the class. One day, he came to me and said it was my turn."

Kendrea's eyes widened. "No way! What did you say?"

"I told him no thanks and kept it moving."

"How preposterous," Kendrea muttered.

"I know," Tiffany nodded. "I was offended and yet flattered at the same time."

Kendrea laughed. "Have you seen him since high school?"

"Yup," Tiffany nodded. "He is still as handsome and still as flirty. He claims I'm the one who got away. I smile and keep it moving—that's community peen now. Probably has a million children all over Jamaica.

"Enough about that. When are we meeting with Kenny and Camden?"

"Tomorrow," Kendrea said. "That's the last meeting, then the rehearsal, then the actual wedding, and then I will be so happy when it's over. I will never volunteer to be the point man at any wedding again."

Tiffany chuckled. "That's right—leave it to the professionals. This reminds me that I want to go over the seating plan with you. Kenny has no time to do this with me. I have a large chart here."

"Yes, sure," Kendrea nodded. "That's what I'm here for. We can go into the kitchen and spread your chart at the breakfast nook."

They headed to the kitchen. Stephanie had her earphones in and was humming while she cooked. It smelled good in there.

"Holy cow," Tiffany whistled. "When you said 'kitchen,' I was expecting a small nook area, not this huge space. This is gorgeous! And there's a view! Is that the chef?"

"Yep," Kendrea said. "That's Stephanie."

"We won't get in her way. She's usually unobtrusive. Stephanie cooks, shares the food, and then leaves."

"I wish I had a chef." Tiffany waved to Stephanie, who waved back. "We used to have a housekeeper growing up, and she used to cook, but the dishes were a hit or miss. To have a dedicated chef would be so freeing. I wouldn't have to worry about what to buy for lunch or what I'm going to eat when I get home."

"It is quite nice," Kendrea nodded.

"Maybe I should throw my hat in the ring for Thomas' affections," Tiffany said slyly.

"I see you have no regard for our friendship," Kendrea growled. "Are you sure you didn't give it up to that Paul guy in high school?"

Tiffany hooted with laughter. "Note to self: never joke about Thomas to Kendrea."

Chapter Fourteen

When Kendrea got up, the morning was chillier than usual. There had been a light drizzle earlier, and the sky was still dark. She wondered if she should join Amanda and Thomas this morning. Her bed was cozy and warm, but she had to go—Thomas worked extra hard when she was around.

Even Amanda had commented on that.

Besides, she couldn't go back to sleep now if she tried; she'd just be tossing and turning. She might as well get up.

She brushed her teeth and combed her hair back into a ponytail. Her keratin treatment was holding up well—her hair was still straight, even in the December humidity. Leaning closer to the mirror, she noticed her skin was glowing. She had never eaten so many vegetables in her life, and Stephanie prepared them in such a way that she didn't even mind. In fact, she now had a craving for roasted carrots—they were that good.

Thomas and Amanda were already on the beach, doing

stretches. Kendrea walked briskly down the stairs. The sun was just beginning to rise, painting the sky with soft pinks and vibrant oranges. The rhythmic sound of waves lapping against the shore filled the air.

She stood still, inhaling it all in.

It was a fabulous day to be alive. She still had to pinch herself sometimes, realizing how privileged she was to live at Ridgeview, with two miles of white sand beach as their backyard.

Thomas waved to her, and she waved back. Amanda had him doing a light jog. She could easily catch up.

"We're doing interval training this morning," Amanda said when Kendrea reached them. "Jogging, then walking."

Kendrea nodded. They usually didn't talk much at the start of their workouts, focusing instead on movement. Amanda had her earphones plugged in, and Thomas breathed heavily, sweat pouring down his face.

He did appear a bit thinner. She blinked rapidly—were her eyes fooling her? No, they weren't. Thomas was making progress. She gave him a thumbs-up.

He responded with a thumbs-down.

"I can hardly haul myself around this morning," he panted.

"That's because you didn't get enough sleep last night," Amanda said. "We talked about this—sleep is integral to weight loss."

Kendrea smirked. "She's right, you know. You're always pushing hard, but your body needs rest too."

Thomas groaned. "Don't remind me." He wiped his forehead with the back of his hand. "I just couldn't sleep. Too much on my mind."

Amanda shot him a sharp look. "What did I say about stress and cortisol levels?"

He rolled his eyes but didn't argue. Instead, he pushed

forward, increasing his pace slightly.

They continued the intervals for another twenty minutes, alternating between jogging and walking. The sun climbed higher, warming their skin despite the lingering coolness in the air. Kendrea felt the burn in her legs, but it was the good kind of pain that came with effort.

When they finally slowed to a stop, Thomas bent over, hands on his knees, catching his breath. "That was brutal."

Amanda grinned. "That was light work. We're leveling up next week and incorporating calisthenics into your routine."

"What's that?" Thomas frowned. "It sounds painful."

Amanda chuckled. "Calisthenics is a fancy word for bodyweight exercises—push-ups, squats, lunges, burpees. We'll even throw in some jump rope."

Thomas groaned. "I knew it sounded painful."

Kendrea laughed. "Come on, you've already come this far. What's a few push-ups?"

He shot her a tired glare. "Easy for you to say. You're not the one dripping sweat like a broken faucet."

"Sweat is good," Amanda said. "It means your body is working. It's a sign of progress."

Thomas groaned dramatically. "It's also a sign that I'm suffering."

Kendrea smirked. "Suffering now, looking good later. Isn't that the deal?"

Amanda nodded. "Exactly. Trust the process. Next week will be your one-month weigh-in, where we'll have an idea of your progress so far."

"There is progress," Thomas said. "I'm going to need to go shopping—most of my pants are loose now."

"Good for you," Kendrea elbowed him.

"I'm going to have to take my tux to the tailor for the wedding. But I'm going to leave it till the last minute, like a day or two before."

"Yes, Thomas, that's real progress," Amanda said, glancing sideways at him with a smile that lingered a moment too long. "Three weeks in, and you're already taking in clothes. It warms my heart."

Thomas chuckled. "This whole weight-loss business isn't as bad as I thought it'd be. I guess I needed you. Thanks for being here."

Amanda's smile widened. "Anytime. You make my job easy—some clients aren't as committed." She brushed a strand of hair away from her face, letting her hand rest on her hip for a moment. "And it's not every day I get to work with someone who's easy on the eyes."

Kendrea coughed pointedly. "I bet she says that to all her clients."

Amanda laughed her tone light and teasing. "No, I do not. Thomas is unmistakably handsome."

She was flirting with him. Kendrea glanced at Thomas, who was smiling like it was the first compliment he had ever gotten in his life. With his disheveled curly hair and sweat-soaked shirt clinging to his frame, he didn't exactly look like a model now, but there was something about him— maybe the way his dimples appeared when he smiled, or the newfound confidence in his posture.

Kendrea raised an eyebrow. "Well, don't let it go to your head, Thomas."

Thomas ran a hand through his damp curls, grinning. "Too late. I think Amanda just made my entire month."

Amanda smirked. "Just stating facts."

Kendrea shook her head, amused but also a little wary. This was new. Amanda was usually all business when it came to training. Thomas had been so focused on getting in shape that flirting hadn't seemed to be on his radar. But now?

She wasn't so sure what was going on.

"Speaking of weddings," Amanda said, "who are you bringing as your date, Kendrea?"

"No one," Kendrea frowned. "I'm the maid of honor; there wouldn't be much time to hang out with a date even if I had one."

She glanced at Thomas, who was looking at her and grinning. "I guess you won't be able to rescue me from Aunt Florence, then?"

Kendrea chuckled. "No."

"I'll rescue you," Amanda said quickly. "If you don't have a date, that is. I love weddings, and I clean up pretty nicely."

Thomas hesitated, glancing between Amanda and Kendrea, who was glaring daggers at Amanda.

The tension in the air was palpable, but Amanda's cheerful tone seemed to cut through it.

"I don't know..." Thomas began.

"Come on, it'll be fun," Amanda coaxed. "And it'll give us a chance to hang out outside of all this sweat and sand. I can even turn it into a lesson on the best things to eat at parties. Just think about it."

Thomas sighed, his lips curling into a reluctant smile. "Alright, fine. You can be my plus-one."

Amanda clapped her hands together, a triumphant grin spreading across her face. "Perfect."

Kendrea, who had been silent until now, finally spoke up, her voice sharp. "Thomas, are you sure that's a good idea? Kenny's wedding is family-focused, not... whatever this is."

Amanda's smile didn't falter, but her tone turned pointed. "Oh, Kendrea, lighten up. I'm just helping out a friend. Besides, don't you want Thomas to enjoy himself?"

Kendrea muttered something under her breath, her

expression stormy.

The rest of the walk continued in strained silence, the sound of the waves doing little to soften the weight of the conversation. Thomas was caught in the middle, focused on the horizon, wondering if he'd made a mistake.

Kendrea was still fuming when she got to work that morning.

Yasmin had texted her earlier to let her know that her building would be ready by the end of December. Kendrea would have a new home for her business in the new year.

"Cool," she texted back to her stepsister. "I can't wait to move in!"

"I'm giving you a family discount, too," Yasmin replied.

"Even cooler," Kendrea responded.

Her frown melted when she saw the figure. It was less than what she was paying now—a nominal sum, really.

"Thank you, Yas," she typed.

Her irritation was well and truly forgotten. She would have new digs soon.

So why was she still bothered by Thomas taking Amanda to the wedding? She had practically begged him to take a date. He hadn't even been enthusiastic about it, but one never knew what could happen at an event filled with romance. Maybe they'd hear a song and start dancing; before they knew it, there was a connection.

Hadn't Thomas said they had a connection when they met at Griffin's wedding?

Good Lord, was she overthinking things?

Probably. But that didn't stop the irritation bubbling up inside her.

Kendrea sighed and tossed her phone onto her desk, rubbing her temples. It wasn't like she had feelings for Thomas.

Did she?

No, of course not.

They were friends.

She was just looking out for him.

Right?

She exhaled sharply and forced herself to focus. She had work to do—two new plans to send to a client who had requested interior design mock-ups in either cooling blue or raging red.

Powering on her laptop, she tried to quell the jealousy gnawing at her when her buzzer went off. She glanced at the door.

It was Dean Gardener?

He knew where she worked?

She pressed the buzzer to let him in, and he smiled.

"Hey, Kendrea."

"Good morning, Dean."

"I had no idea I'd find you here," Dean said. "I took a chance and dropped by."

"I rarely get drop-bys," Kendrea replied. "Especially in this plaza. But I just got word that I'll be moving soon—to Sterling Plaza."

"Oh yes," Dean nodded. "But of course, you'll be moving to Thomas' building."

"Nope, not Thomas' building," Kendrea shook her head. "His sister Yasmin's building. Newly built and twice as spacious. Ooh, I can't wait."

Dean chuckled.

"So, what brings you by?" Kendrea asked.

"I have a job," Dean said. "And you come highly recommended. I'm friends with Amanda, and she can't stop gushing over how good a job you did with the place she's staying. She sent me pictures, and I was impressed."

"You know Amanda Pierce?"

"I do," Dean said. "Met her at Mingles, actually. She's a great person. Unfortunately, she's in a relationship already."

"She is?" Kendrea frowned. "I had no idea."

"Well, anyway," Dean continued, "the job is for my mother. She's currently custom-building what she calls her vacation house. As you know, she lives in Canada. It's a three-bedroom bungalow in a gated community. If you squint a little, there's a decent sea view. She wants it professionally done so she can offer it as a place to stay when she's not there."

"So, like an Airbnb type of thing?"

"Exactly," Dean nodded. "But right now, it's just an empty shell. We're at the stage where I need to choose tiles, paint, and all of that, and I'd really like to consult someone with an eye for detail."

Kendrea rubbed her hands together, excitement beginning to replace the irritation from earlier. "I'll need to see the space to get a proper feel for what's needed. When are you thinking of starting?"

Dean smiled, clearly pleased she was interested. "As soon as possible. The builders are wrapping up the last bits of structural work, so it's the perfect time to start styling the interior. I can take you there this weekend if you're available."

Kendrea nodded. "That works for me. Just send me the location and a time that suits you, and I'll meet you there."

"Great. I'll text you the details later today."

Dean's easygoing manner put her at ease. For the first time that morning, she found herself genuinely looking forward to something.

"So, do you have a particular vision in mind, or is your mom giving me free rein to work my magic?" Kendrea asked, tilting her head with a curious smile.

Dean chuckled. "My mom definitely has opinions, but she trusts professionals. I think she'd be open to your ideas, as long as it feels warm and welcoming. She's got that classic Caribbean charm in mind but doesn't want it to feel too dated or touristy."

"Got it," Kendrea said, already forming ideas. "I'll take some pictures, plug the designs into my software, and she can choose whatever floats her boat."

Dean nodded. "Thanks, Kendrea. I appreciate you taking this on. Considering our breakup and all, I didn't think you'd be up for it. So this is what being amicable with an ex feels like."

Kendrea chuckled. "You've never been friendly with an ex before?"

"Nope," Dean shook his head. "Usually, we just go our separate ways and never speak again."

Kendrea smirked. "Well, consider this your first successful post-breakup friendship."

Dean grinned. "I guess so. Though, to be fair, you're probably the only ex I'd actually want to be friends with. I've never managed to be friends with the opposite sex, but maybe I'll finally figure out what's going on with you and Thomas. Your relationship has always baffled me."

"Oh, stop," Kendrea said.

Dean gave her a pointed look. "He's the reason we broke up. The one thing that was wrong with me was that I wasn't Thomas."

"Not true," Kendrea said faintly.

"It is true," Dean shrugged. "You had Thomas to fulfill all your needs in a relationship. He was the one you called with good news, bad news—anything in between. You spoke to him more than you did with me. The only thing we had going was sex. And even then, you always held back. I got the feeling you wanted to be somewhere else. Maybe in his arms." He tilted his head. "What's the real reason you two aren't going at it like rabbits?"

Kendrea inhaled sharply. "My relationship with Thomas is none of your business."

"I know," Dean nodded. "But I'm madly curious about his hold over you."

Kendrea folded her arms, her jaw tightening. "He doesn't have a hold over me, Dean. We're just close. Guys and girls can be close without ulterior motives."

Dean huffed out a dry laugh. "Close is an understatement. You and I were together for over a year, and I still felt like an outsider in whatever world you and Thomas share."

She looked away, exhaling slowly. "I don't know what you want me to say."

"Try the truth," he said, softer this time. "You want to be with him. What's holding you back?"

Kendrea hesitated. That was the million-dollar question, wasn't it? What was holding her back?

She could list a dozen reasons off the top of her head but top of the list was the possibility that they'd ruin their friendship. She wasn't going to risk losing the one person who'd been her constant friend through the years.

However, none of those reasons explained why her stomach twisted every time she thought about him with Amanda.

She lifted her chin. "Thomas and I work because we aren't together. He's my best friend, and that's enough for me."

Dean studied her, then shook his head with a knowing smile. "You sure about that?"

Kendrea swallowed hard. "Yes."

He nodded slowly, but the smirk on his face told her he

didn't believe her for a second.

Chapter Fifteen

"**A**bout this morning," Thomas said as soon as she walked in through the front door. "I didn't mean to invite Amanda to the wedding."

"It's fine," Kendrea said. "She practically begged you to take her. I was there—I saw how she manipulated the invite."

"It's not fine," Thomas said. "If looks could kill, you would have killed me this morning when I invited her as my plus-one."

"I was just wondering how easy it was for her to do it," Kendrea said. "But it's all good. I ended up having a great day. I'll be moving to Sterling Plaza for the new year. Yasmin's building is done, and I have a new job. The kind of job I like. I get to choose the paints, the tiles, and the trimmings on a new construction."

Thomas looked at her, troubled. "So you're not mad that I'm taking Amanda to Kenny's wedding?"

"Nope," Kendrea said, heading to the kitchen. "Did Stephanie leave my dinner?"

"But of course," Thomas said. "I feel like you're taking this too well."

"It's just a date to a wedding," Kendrea said flippantly. "Maybe I should invite someone."

"No, Kendrea." Thomas shook his head. "I knew this would be your revenge."

Kendrea stopped mid-step, turning to face him with an arched brow. "Revenge? Seriously? It's just a date to a wedding, Thomas. No biggie."

Thomas groaned, running a hand through his hair. "You're way too calm about this. It's unsettling. You don't get over stuff like this that easily."

"Maybe I'm growing as a person," she teased, opening the fridge to pull out her neatly packed dinner. "Or maybe I just have better things to focus on, like moving to my new space and this project I landed. Dean Gardener's mom wants me to design her vacation home—a three-bedroom bungalow with a great sea view. It's right up my alley."

"Dean Gardener?" Thomas narrowed his eyes. "As in your former fiancé?"

Kendrea rolled her eyes, and put her food in the microwave. "That Dean Gardener. He was polite and businesslike, which is more than I can say for you and Amanda with your little beach flirtations. What was happening this morning? She's getting bold."

Thomas crossed his arms, leaning against the counter. "So, you're telling me Dean just randomly shows up at your work with a big project, and there's no ulterior motive? You don't see how that might be a little suspicious?"

She shrugged. "Dean's a nice guy, and his mom's project sounds amazing. If there's an ulterior motive, that's his business. I'm focused on the job."

Thomas narrowed his eyes at her. "Focused, huh? So if he just so happens to ask to be your plus-one for Kenny's wedding, you're saying you won't go?"

Kendrea smirked, leaning on the counter. "Well, now that you mention it, it would be a nice way to rub your little date with Amanda in your face."

"See? Revenge!" Thomas pointed at her like he'd won a prize.

She laughed, shaking her head. "You're ridiculous. Look, I don't need to get revenge on you, Thomas. You're already stuck going to a wedding with someone who is clearly interested in you. The term 'gold digger' comes to mind."

"That's harsh," Thomas muttered, though the flicker of doubt in his eyes suggested she'd hit a nerve. "Amanda is not like Nicole or any of the other gold diggers I've known. She's genuine and sweet."

Kendrea raised an eyebrow, crossing her arms. "Genuine and sweet? Right. The girl who bullied you in high school, who is now suddenly complimenting you on being handsome? She wants something. They always want something."

Thomas frowned, his jaw tightening. "That's not fair. Amanda's been nothing but kind to me, and she's not exactly hurting for money herself. She doesn't need anything from me."

Kendrea smirked, tilting her head. "Oh, come on. You're a walking, talking jackpot, Thomas. Trust me, I've seen this game before."

He ran a hand through his hair, visibly frustrated. "You're just projecting because you don't like Amanda. She's been helping me get back into shape and supporting me through all of this. I don't see why you have to twist it into something it's not."

"Supporting you?" Kendrea asked, her voice dripping with sarcasm. "By flirting with you during every workout? Please, Thomas. You're not blind. And don't even try to pretend you don't enjoy the attention."

Thomas opened his mouth to respond but stopped, his expression softening slightly. "Maybe I do enjoy it," he admitted after a pause. "But that doesn't mean her intentions are bad. Not everyone's out to get me, Kendrea."

She sighed, shaking her head as she took a bite of her food. "Fine, Thomas. If you believe Amanda is the real deal, then great. Have fun at the wedding and whatever else she has planned for you. Just don't come crying to me when she shows her true colors."

"And what about Dean?" Thomas countered, his tone sharp. "You're so quick to judge Amanda, but you're ready to team up with Dean Gardener on a project and play nice? How do you know he doesn't have some ulterior motive?"

Kendrea smirked, unfazed. "If Dean has ulterior motives, I'm not interested. I broke it off with him for a reason. What we had wasn't working. I have no desire to be in a relationship with him again. You, on the other hand, are setting yourself up for drama with Amanda. You did say you two had a connection. But I'll be there with popcorn when it all blows up."

Thomas groaned, throwing his hands up in frustration. "You're impossible."

"And you're predictable," she shot back, putting her plate on the counter. She wasn't even hungry anymore. "Enjoy your 'genuine and sweet' Amanda. I'll enjoy watching the show. You know what? I'm going to bed."

Before she could walk away, Thomas pulled her to him from behind.

"Why are we like this?" he whispered in her ear. "What's wrong with us?"

Kendrea spun around, wrapped her arms around his neck, and reached for his lips. The kiss was ravenous, full of unspoken frustrations, of years of tension neither of them had dared to name. Thomas responded instantly, his hands gripping her waist, pulling her flush against him. It was reckless and heated—like a dam finally breaking.

Kendrea's fingers tangled in his curls, and for a moment, she let herself drown in it. In him.

Then reality slammed into her.

She pulled away, breathless, her lips tingling. "Thomas…"

His forehead rested against hers, his chest rising and falling. "You can't tell me that was nothing."

She stepped back, shaking her head. "That's the problem. It's not nothing. And if we cross that line, there's no going back."

He exhaled, running a hand down his face. "Maybe going back isn't what we need."

Her heart clenched, but she forced herself to stand her ground. "You're taking Amanda to Kenny's wedding."

Thomas frowned. "She practically begged me to."

"And you went along with it." Her voice was quieter now. "Look, I know you haven't had much luck with women, but you are losing weight now, and pretty soon, you'll be looking like their ideal. It may get to your head, and I really don't want to stand in your way while you explore. I don't want to be hurt in the process; that would destroy us for good. I can't deal with that."

"What on earth are you going on about?" Thomas asked, puzzled.

"I'm just saying," Kendrea swallowed. "You will change. Your way of looking at life will evolve. People's reactions to you will also evolve. You might think you want me now, but in the future, you may not. And I don't want that kind of drama in my life. It's better to just be friends. If you hurt me, it will be catastrophic. I would lose you."

"Where is all of this nonsense coming from?" Thomas frowned. "I will love you, and I want you, whether I am thick or thin. And I would never knowingly hurt you. That would be like hurting myself."

"You don't know that," Kendrea said.

"I do know how I feel," Thomas said. "It's a constant emotion that's been a part of me since I was in my teens. I also know that my weight loss or gain will not change my feelings towards you. How much longer are we going to pretend that we're just best friends when we're clearly something else?"

"I don't know," Kendrea said.

A muscle ticked in his jaw. "What do you really want, Kendrea?"

"I want to ignore this thing between us for as long as I can," Kendrea said honestly.

Thomas exhaled sharply, shaking his head. "That's not an answer. That's avoidance."

She crossed her arms, looking away. "Maybe it is. But it's safer."

"For who?" he demanded. "Because it sure as hell doesn't feel safe to me. It feels like torture."

Kendrea closed her eyes for a moment, willing herself to be rational, to not give in to the pull between them. "I can't risk losing you, Thomas."

His hands found her arms, gentle but firm. "You're pushing me away because you're scared. But I'm right here, and I'm not going anywhere. So stop acting like I'm some unpredictable variable in your life."

She huffed out a breath, her chest tight with emotions she wasn't ready to name. "I just don't want to wake up one day and realize that I was just a phase for you."

His grip tightened slightly. "A phase? Kendrea, I've loved you since before I even knew what love was. There's nothing temporary about this."

She stared up at him, searching his face for any trace of hesitation. There was none. Just unwavering certainty.

The truth was, she wanted him, too—she always had. But wanting him meant risking everything, and that terrified her.

"Just give me time," she whispered. "I need time to figure this out."

Thomas studied her for a long moment, then sighed, releasing his hold. "Fine. Take all the time you need." He stepped back, his eyes shadowed. "But don't take too long, Kendrea. Because I'm done pretending."

And with that, he turned and walked away, leaving her standing there, feeling like the ground beneath her had just cracked open.

Chapter Sixteen

It was the morning of the wedding and Kendrea was getting ready with her sisters at Kenny's townhouse. It was a beehive of activity. Kenice was contorting Kenny's hair into a gorgeous updo, all while complaining that Kenny should have straightened her hair because it would have been easier.

"Your hair has gotten so long, it's almost Kendrea's length. You could have straightened it and flaunted it for your big day."

"No thanks," Kenny said. "I don't want to risk heat damage for a day. Besides, Camden loves my natural hair. Do the style and stop complaining."

Kenisha, who was doing her nails, chuckled. "Complainer."

"No bickering today, Kenice and Kenisha," Kendrea said sternly. She was running the steamer over all the dresses. "Today we are zen."

"If I'm not going to bicker with Kenisha," Kenice asked,

"what else is there to do?"

"Listen to the soothing music in the background," Kendrea said. "Fields of Gold by Sting just puts you in the mood for a wedding."

"It is a nice song," Kenice said. "I love the chronology of it: they meet, they fall in love, they get old, and they die together among the fields of barley. Their love was so strong it made the sun jealous."

"Make the sun jealous with your love for Camden, Kenny," Kenice sniffed.

"Stop!" Kendrea said exasperatedly. "No crying."

"I can't bicker with Kenisha; I can't cry when thinking of Kenny's happiness," Kenice muttered. "What on earth should I do?"

"Discuss her hot and heavy romance with Thomas," Kenisha snickered.

"There is no hot and heavy romance with Thomas," Kendrea snorted. "He is taking his health coach as his plus one to the wedding. She clearly manipulated him into doing it right in front of my face. And I'm wondering, is Thomas short a brain cell? Why is he so easily malleable with these women?"

They all chuckled.

"He is smart," Kenice said. "Quite so."

"How do you figure?" Kendrea asked heatedly.

"You're bursting with jealousy about the situation," Kenice said. "It's the game you two play with each other. It's getting tiring."

"I am not playing any games," Kendrea said. "If I were, I would have taken someone as my plus one and driven him crazy and see how he would feel about that."

"Mmm, is that maturity I smell?" Kenny chuckled.

"Nope, it's my Chanel No. 5," Kendrea snorted. "Some of

it spilled in my bag."

"You know what I mean," Kenny said. "You and Thomas play games with each other. You date someone, he dates someone."

"And the cycle goes on," Kenice said. "I'm bored. We need another trope. Sleep with the man already and put him out of his misery. You know you want to."

Kendrea rolled her eyes. "You're all so annoying. I'm not sleeping with Thomas."

Kenisha smirked. "Not yet."

"Not ever, no matter how much I want to," Kendrea insisted, setting the steamer down with more force than necessary. "When I do, it will change everything. I don't like changes."

"We know," Kenice and Kenisha said in unison.

Kenny laughed. "You two rehearsed that?"

Kenisha grinned. "Nope. We just know our sister."

Kendrea sighed, crossing her arms. "I don't see why this is such a big deal to you all. I'm perfectly fine with how things are between me and Thomas."

Kenice snorted. "Sure, that's why you're so bothered by the health coach."

"I am not bothered," Kendrea hissed.

"Liar," Kenisha giggled. "You are so bothered, it hurts."

Kenny shook her head, amused. "Look, whatever's going on with you and Thomas, it'll sort itself out. Today, the focus is on me. I'm getting married, in case you all forgot."

Kendrea exhaled sharply. "Yes, exactly. That's what we should be talking about. Not me. Not Thomas. Just you and Camden."

Kenice finished pinning the last section of Kenny's hair and stepped back to admire her work. "Well, there. Your hair's done, nails are almost done, the dress is steamed…

and we still have time to kill."

Kenisha grinned. "Which means we can go back to discussing Kendrea's love life."

"No, we cannot." Kendrea grabbed a throw pillow and tossed it at her.

****

"I would paint this," Kendrea whispered to herself. She was admiring Cloud Nine Inn's beauty. The view was quite similar to Ridgeview's, but something about the azure blue of the Caribbean Sea stretching out endlessly before her, kissed by the golden hues of the evening sun, made her feel poetic.

The soothing sounds of the saxophonist in the background, fit the mood perfectly as he played Kenny G's Forever in Love.

The breeze was gentle enough not to be a nuisance. She lined up by the gazebo with her sisters, and Audra and Jewel, Kenny's best friends. A scattering of red roses framed the intimate ceremony space.

George walked Kenny down the aisle to the evocative notes of Kenny G's Wedding Song. Kendrea blinked back tears. It was quite emotional. Her eyes caught Thomas's; he was staring right at her, not at the advancing bride.

He had an enigmatic expression on his face. What was he thinking? She wondered.

She knew the moment he realized that she was aware of his gaze. He smiled at her slowly.

Her heart fluttered, and her breath hitched. That smile—lazy, confident, and knowing—made her pulse quicken. Thomas's way of looking at her unsettled her as if he saw straight through her carefully composed exterior. She quickly turned her gaze back to Kenny, who was radiant as she walked toward Camden.

The love between them was palpable, an unspoken promise in the way they looked at each other. The golden hour sun bathed them in warm color tones, making the moment feel even more surreal. Kendrea stole another glance at Thomas. He was still watching her. Her eyes shifted to Amanda sitting beside him. She had been so caught up in Thomas's unwavering gaze that she had forgotten that Amanda was his date.

The officiant's voice pulled her back to the present, and she focused on Kenny and Camden as they exchanged vows. But even as the ceremony continued, a quiet awareness settled over her.

Thomas wasn't just looking at her. He was speaking with his eyes, compelling her to listen. And what was he saying? I want you, and I know you want me too.

Kendrea inhaled and released her breath slowly. She really did want him, but she wasn't sure what was stopping her from taking the next step.

She pressed her lips together, forcing herself to focus on the moment—the vows, the love radiating between Kenny and Camden, the way the light danced off the water. This was a wedding, a celebration of commitment, not the time to get lost in the intensity of Thomas's gaze.

But it was difficult. Especially when, from the corner of her eye, she caught the way Amanda leaned in to whisper something to him. Thomas nodded absently, his gaze flickering to her only briefly before returning to Kendrea, his expression unreadable.

She should look away.

She should remind herself that he wasn't hers.

And yet, that wasn't entirely true, was it?

Not in the way he looked at her. Not in the way her body responded instinctively, her pulse quickening as if it already knew what her mind refused to admit.

The applause brought her back.

Kenny and Camden kissed, sealing their vows, and the guests erupted in cheers. Kendrea clapped, smiling as Kenny beamed at her new husband, but she was acutely aware of Thomas standing just a few feet away.

As the newlyweds made their way back down the aisle, arms wrapped around each other, and the bridal party broke up into groups for pictures, Kendrea felt a warm breath at her ear.

"You're overthinking it, Drea."

Thomas.

Her heart nearly leaped from her chest, but she didn't turn to face him. She didn't have to—she could feel his presence, feel the heat of him so close.

Kendrea swallowed hard, steeling herself before finally turning her head and meeting his eyes again. And in that single, charged moment, she knew—whatever this was between them, it wasn't going away. Not tonight. Not ever.

"You look stunning, by the way," he said, smiling. "I couldn't take my eyes off you."

Kendrea chuckled softly. "You look stunning too."

Thomas laughed, the sound light and genuine. "I've never been described as stunning."

"Well, I am stunned when I look at you, trying to reconcile the Thomas of a month ago with the man standing before me now." Kendrea chuckled. "I'm really proud of you, you know that?"

"I know." Thomas took a step closer, the space between them shrinking, and Kendrea felt a warmth spread through her chest. He gently brushed a stray lock of hair behind her ear. The touch was electric, and Kendrea's breath caught in her throat.

"I've been thinking about your fear of changing things between us," Thomas said gently. "And a quote came to me. I don't even remember who wrote it, but it goes: Accept what is, let go of what was, and have faith in what will be."

Kendrea exhaled slowly, her heart pounding. Thomas had always been smooth, but this wasn't just charm—this was him, real and unguarded.

"Have faith in what will be," she echoed softly, tasting the words on her lips.

His eyes searched hers, waiting. For what, she wasn't entirely sure. Permission? A sign?

Amanda's laughter rang out from somewhere behind them, a stark reminder that he hadn't come here alone. That whatever was happening between them—whatever had always been simmering beneath the surface—was still undefined.

Kendrea swallowed. "And what exactly will be, Thomas?"

He smiled, slow and knowing. "That's up to you."

The space between them felt smaller than it should, as if the air itself was conspiring to draw them together. She could still feel the warmth of his fingertips where he had tucked her hair behind her ear, as if he'd left a mark on her skin.

"You're making this difficult," she admitted, her voice barely above a whisper.

Thomas tilted his head, considering her words. "Or maybe I'm making it simple."

She let out a quiet laugh, shaking her head. "You always think you have the answers, don't you?"

His grin widened. "Not always. But I know this—I want you, Kendrea. I have for a long time."

Her breath caught.

This time, he wasn't hiding behind teasing remarks or playful flirtation. His words settled deep inside her, undeniable and real.

The photographer called for the bridesmaids, breaking the moment, and Kendrea took a step back, trying to regain her balance.

"Looks like I have to go," she murmured.

Thomas nodded but didn't move away. "For now. Save a dance for me later."

****

"I can see it now," Kenice said in wonderment behind her as they arranged themselves for the picture.

"See what?" Kendrea asked, puzzled.

"Why you have been tormented about Thomas," Kenice whispered. "There is something about him that's appealing; it's almost magnetic. Look at Amanda drooling over your man like a dog in heat."

Kendrea sighed. "Kenice, if you are trying to make me jealous, it's not working. Thomas has always been that way."

"Only you thought so. The fat was hiding his light," Kenice chuckled. "Now that he is losing weight, it's coming out. I think if you keep fooling around, you'll lose him to an opportunist like Amanda."

Kendrea stiffened, forcing a smile as the photographer gestured for them to get closer. "Kenice, Thomas isn't mine to lose."

Kenice scoffed. "Girl, please. He's been yours."

Kendrea turned her attention to the camera, pretending she hadn't heard, but her sister's words lingered. She wasn't wrong. Thomas had always been hers in some way, but had she really allowed herself to claim him?

"Alright, big smiles!" the photographer called.

Kendrea plastered on a grin. Kenice nudged her. "You don't have to say anything now, but think about it. If you don't step up, someone else will."

As the shutter clicked, Kendrea inhaled deeply. She didn't need Kenice to tell her that. She already knew. And the question that haunted her wasn't whether Thomas was hers. It was whether she was brave enough to finally be his.

Chapter Seventeen

It was amazing how time marched on whether or not you were doing something with it. Thomas looked at himself in the gym mirror. It was weigh-in day, month two. He had an audience behind him as he stepped on the scale—Amanda, Stephanie, and Kendrea were all looking at the number with differing expressions of shock.

He had a moment of pride himself. He had not lapsed, not even once, into his old eating habits, and he had gotten used to getting up and exercising. He had more energy, felt different. He looked at the scale as well.

"I can't believe it," Kendrea whispered. "Twenty pounds in a month, that's amazing."

"Beyond expectations!" Amanda walked over to him and hugged him. "That's thirty-five pounds in two months. That's four whole pounds a week on average. That's more than I would have hoped. You are a dream client."

He didn't like the way her voice softened when she said

"dream." He didn't hug her back. She was getting a bit too handsy lately. He gave her a brief pat on the back and stepped away as quickly as possible.

Kendrea also moved towards him for a hug, and Amanda stepped back.

She slid into his arms like she was supposed to be there, her head resting on his heart. He wrapped his hands around her. Any excuse for bodily contact was fine by him. He was still a little chuffed that he hadn't made headway with Kendrea at Kenny and Camden's wedding. She was still keeping him at arm's length. This month was a study in patience for him.

"You really do feel thinner, and are those muscles I feel?" Kendrea chuckled, bringing him back to the present.

He didn't want her to move away; he tightened his arms when she made to leave.

"So I, er, was thinking that we should celebrate," Amanda said brightly. "You take us to dinner this evening, all three of us."

Still hanging on to Kendrea, he looked over at Amanda. "Sure."

"I can't this evening," Kendrea groaned, easing away from his arms. "I have a delivery at a client's house. I need to be there for that."

He wondered if the client was Dean. They didn't speak about him, and he wasn't going to ask. He was curious, though.

"And I have a date with a guy I met at the market," Stephanie said, "but here is your two-month gift."

It was a book. Thomas took it from her.

"It has all of your favorite recipes and how to make them," Stephanie said. "I will be available for classes whenever you feel like it."

"I'd be down for that," Kendrea said eagerly.

Stephanie nodded. "I have to go prep breakfast. Congrats again, Thomas."

"Ah," Amanda said, "sounds like it will be just you and me for dinner then."

Thomas looked at Kendrea. "Are you sure you can't make it?"

"Quite sure," Kendrea nodded. After the delivery, I am going to check out my new office location and see how best to decorate it."

Amanda clapped her hands triumphantly.

Thomas sighed inwardly. Amanda was persistent, and he didn't want to be rude, but he also didn't want to give her the wrong idea. He shot a final look at Kendrea, hoping for some miraculous change of heart, but she was already backing out of the room, looking wholly unbothered.

"Alright then," he said reluctantly. "Guess it's just us. Meet me at the office; we'll decide where to go from there."

Amanda beamed, slipping her arm through his. "It'll be fun," she said, steering him toward the bench press machine. "My treat since you're the star of the show."

Thomas didn't argue, though he wasn't particularly looking forward to a one-on-one dinner with her.

He glanced over his shoulder in time to catch Kendrea watching them, a slight crease between her brows before she turned away.

Interesting. So she was bothered. That warmed his heart.

****

"I can't believe I gave up dinner for this," Kendrea muttered. All day she had been in a bad mood. She imagined that Amanda was sinking her tentacles into Thomas, whispering how much of a dream client he was.

The delivery driver was stuck in traffic because of an accident, and Dean himself was late. She sat in the driveway, feeling hungrier and hungrier as the minutes rolled by. She wondered where Thomas would take Amanda for dinner and what they would eat.

A knock on the car window made her jump.

She rolled down the window. It was Dean.

"Sorry I'm late," he said. "The traffic is horrific on that side of town. I think there was an accident."

"That's what the delivery driver said," Kendrea opened her car door, and he sat down.

"Whew, it's crazy out there," Dean murmured. "I almost stopped the car in the middle of the gridlock and got something to eat. We were moving that slow."

"I was just thinking about food, too," Kendrea said. "I could eat some kimchi right now."

"I never understood why you liked it so much," Dean chuckled. "I never liked cabbage, whether it's fermented or not."

"The first time I had it, I went over to Thomas' house. His grandmother made it. I initially hesitated to try it, but trust me when I tell you that Thomas' granny knows how to cook. That kimchi remains the best I've ever tasted, bar none. Lori claims she does the recipe exactly as her grandmother did it, but bless her heart, hers cannot come close to that recipe."

Dean chuckled. "You really do sound hungry."

"I could eat two whole cabbages," Kendrea said longingly. "And a chicken, and some rice, and maybe half of a cow."

"And I'd join you," Dean said, looking at his watch. "Do you want us to go grab something and then come back here?"

"Is there a restaurant near here?" Kendrea asked. "Because I'm not venturing back into the town area until rush-hour traffic is over."

"There's a hotel near here, Sea Caves. They offer a buffet service, all-you-can-eat. A mutual friend of ours suggested that I try it."

"Which mutual friend?" Kendrea asked.

"Amanda," Dean said. "She seems to really like you. Your name comes up in every conversation."

"Oh really?" Kendrea frowned.

"Yup," Dean said. "She seems to think you're great, fantastic, and that you and I should get back together. I wasn't considering it because I know Thomas would be a third wheel in our relationship again, but then again, why not? It's not like you have something going on with him. Amanda says you two are genuinely just friends. I still can't fathom it."

"Wait a minute," Kendrea frowned. "No, I'm not interested in getting back with you, but I am too hungry to think about Amanda discussing me with you. Where is the restaurant?"

"At the bottom of the hill, just two minutes away. They recently opened to the public," Dean said. "I've been meaning to check it out. If the delivery guy gets here, we can make a dash back without him having to wait on us."

"Okay, cool." Kendrea nodded.

"We can travel in my car," Dean said. "I know where it is."

"And no talk of getting back together," Kendrea said. "Trust me when I tell you, that horse has gone far past the gate and is never coming back. Been there, done that, bought the ticket, saw the show, and realized it wasn't worth the hype."

"Okay, okay," Dean shrugged. "That's what I thought."

Chapter Eighteen

Thomas was having a chill moment in the restaurant, listening to the soothing music—Ice and Fire by King Cannon. Somehow, the melody reminded him of Kendrea, and for a moment, his mind wandered to her, completely tuning out the bright chatter from Amanda, who was in the middle of telling him a story about her childhood.

Two months ago, if you had told him that he would be sitting in a buffet restaurant with Amanda Pierce from high school—who was flirting with him madly—and that his belly had somehow shrunken enough so that it wasn't touching the table, he would have laughed.

He would have laughed even harder if you'd told him it was an all-you-can-eat buffet and that his plate was mostly filled with vegetables and just two proteins.

"Oh look, it's Kendrea and her boyfriend, Dean," Amanda said, cutting into his thoughts.

Thomas froze, his fork hovering midway to his mouth.

His eyes flicked toward the entrance before he could stop himself. And there she was—Kendrea, looking effortlessly stunning in a fitted dress, her hair loose and flirting with her waist. Dean stood beside her, a hand at the small of her back as they spoke to the hostess.

Boyfriend.

The word bounced around in his head. They aren't together. This is just dinner. He told himself he didn't care, but the tightening in his chest told a different story.

Amanda smirked, watching his reaction. "Huh. Didn't know she was dating him officially. Guess that explains why she was too busy to come to dinner with us."

Thomas didn't respond. He took a slow bite of his food, chewing mechanically as he watched the hostess lead Kendrea and Dean to a table on the opposite side of the restaurant.

He told himself to look away—told himself he was overreacting. But when Dean pulled out Kendrea's chair for her, and she smiled up at him—really smiled—Thomas felt something bitter creep up his throat.

Amanda, ever perceptive, leaned in slightly. "You good?"

"Fine," he said, a little too quickly.

She let out a soft chuckle. "You know, if you're trying to play it cool, you're failing."

Thomas shot her a dry look. "Eat your food, Amanda."

She grinned but did as told. Meanwhile, Thomas fought the urge to glance across the room again. There was nothing going on between them. He had no reason to care. No reason to be bothered.

And yet...

The night suddenly felt a lot less chill.

****

He didn't feel like going home. He paced his apartment like a caged lion. Jealousy was coursing through him like lava.

Kendrea was back with Dean Gardener. She had lied to him and made him think that the two of them were just working together.

Why was he mad? Kendrea and he were just friends. He was beginning to hate those two words, just friends. It was a lie when applied to him and Kendrea. He was tired of this cat-and-mouse game they were involved in. He had been too patient with her, allowing her to put him at arm's length. No more. Things were going to be laid out between them tonight.

He drove home like a mad man, tortured by his thoughts. There were no lights on in the house, only the security ones. She was probably not there; she was probably with Dean.

He walked up the stairs, his feet heavy, but then he saw a light under her bedroom door.

It was the only encouragement he needed. He knocked once and twice, then decided he didn't care if he was being rude and tried the handle. It wasn't locked.

Kendrea curled up in bed with her laptop and looked up in surprise. "Thomas?"

His pulse pounded. She was home. Not with Dean.

"Didn't think you'd be here," he said, stepping inside and shutting the door behind him.

She arched a brow. "Where else would I be?"

He let out a short laugh, one with no humor. "Out with your boyfriend."

Kendrea's brow furrowed. "Excuse me?"

"Dean. Your boyfriend. You know, your ex or current, who knows what's going on. You didn't mention that you didn't want to go to dinner with me and Amanda because you were going with him."

Her mouth parted, then shut, and for a moment, she just stared at him. Then, to his absolute frustration, she started laughing.

"Oh my God," she said, shaking her head. "You're jealous."

Thomas clenched his jaw. "I'm pissed off."

"No, you're jealous," she repeated, sitting up and folding her arms. "And you're being ridiculous. I am not seeing Dean again that ship has sailed."

That threw him for a second, but he wasn't about to be sidetracked. "Looked like it tonight."

She sighed, rubbing a hand down her face. "The delivery guy was late, and we were hungry. He suggested the buffet. Why didn't you come over and say hello? We could have joined you and Amanda."

He exhaled hard through his nose. "You really expect me to believe there's nothing going on between you two?"

Kendrea stared at him for a long moment. Then, with an unreadable expression, she said, "Why do you care?"

That was the moment. The line in the sand. He could back off, play it cool, pretend he wasn't standing here, breathing heavily in her bedroom like a man on the edge.

Or he could tell the truth.

"I care," he said, his voice rough, "because I want you, I love you, and I don't want you to be with anyone else."

There was silence.

His heart pounded as he watched her reaction, waiting for her to push him away. Tell him he was reading too much into things.

Instead, Kendrea slowly closed her laptop and slid out of bed, standing right in front of him.

"Then do something about it," she murmured.

And just like that, patience was a thing of the past.

Thomas didn't need to be told twice. The moment the words left Kendrea's lips, he reached for her, his hands settling on her waist as he pulled her against him. She fit against him perfectly, like she was meant to be there.

He kissed her—hard, deep like he'd been starving for this moment. And in a way, he had. Two months of patience, of waiting for her to stop holding him at arm's length, all of it snapped under the weight of his need.

Kendrea wasn't passive. She met him kiss for kiss, her fingers threading through his hair, tugging just enough to send a sharp thrill through him. She tasted sweet, familiar, but new all at once.

His hands roamed, memorizing every curve through the thin fabric of her sleepwear. She was so damn soft, warm, and when he slid his hands beneath the hem of her tank top, her breath hitched against his lips.

"Thomas," she murmured, her nails grazing his shoulders as he guided them toward the bed.

"Say it again," he rasped, trailing kisses down her neck, exploring the sensitive spot beneath her jaw.

She exhaled a shaky breath, fingers tightening in his hair. "Thomas."

A rush of satisfaction coursed through him. He needed more.

He peeled her tank top upward with steady hands, giving her time to stop him if she wanted. She didn't. She lifted her arms, letting him pull it over her head, and the sight of her, bare and wanting, nearly undid him.

"Damn," he murmured, running his hands down her sides, watching the way her skin prickled under his touch.

Kendrea reached for his shirt in return, dragging it up his torso. He helped her, yanking it over his head before pressing his body against hers once more. The heat between them was electric, the tension finally breaking into something undeniable.

Their kisses deepened and turned urgent. Hands roamed, exploring, claiming. Thomas wasn't just touching her—he was learning her, savoring every reaction, every sharp inhale, every way she pressed closer as if she wanted to crawl inside his skin.

There was no hesitation, no doubt. Just the two of them, tangled in each other, finally giving in.

And this time, he wasn't letting her slip away.

Chapter Nineteen

Life is a flow of natural and spontaneous changes. Don't resist them. Let things flow naturally forward in whatever way you like.

Kendrea read the quote and smiled to herself. She had been doing just that since she and Thomas had stopped pretending that they were just friends. She had all but moved into his room. They had seamlessly moved into a new sort of relationship, and they tacitly didn't discuss it or define it.

Outwardly, neither of them had changed much. They still exercised in the mornings, they worked at the same location, they had dinner together at night, they watched movies together—albeit sometimes the movie ended up watching them—and they couldn't get enough of each other.

But they didn't talk about it.

Kendrea told herself she was fine with that. They had an understanding. There were no labels, no expectations, just them—wrapped up in each other, sharing space, sharing bodies, sharing everything except words.

And yet…

She closed the book she had been reading, staring at the cover without really seeing it.

Thomas walked in from the shower, a towel slung low around his hips, steam still clinging to his skin. He shot her a lazy grin, rubbing another towel through his damp hair. "What's with the face?"

She blinked. "What face?"

"That one." He dropped onto the bed beside her, tilting her chin toward him. "The overthinking face."

Kendrea scoffed. "I do not have an overthinking face."

"You do." He kissed the corner of her mouth. "It's cute."

She sighed, letting herself lean into him for a moment before pulling back. "Thomas… what are we doing?"

He stilled, his smile fading just a little.

"Living," he said simply. "Enjoying each other. Not overcomplicating things."

Kendrea searched his face. "And you're okay with that?"

"Are you?"

She hesitated.

He let out a breath, running a hand through his hair. "Kendrea, if you want to talk about this, we can. But I thought we were happy."

"We are," she admitted. And that was the problem. It was too good. Too easy. She was waiting for the other shoe to drop.

He studied her for a long moment before pulling her onto his lap and cradling her against his chest. "Tell me what's on your mind."

She sighed, pressing her forehead against his shoulder. "I don't know," she murmured. "Maybe I'm just waiting for something to go wrong."

Thomas's hand moved slowly up and down her back, grounding her, soothing her. "Why would it?"

She huffed out a small, humorless laugh. "Because things don't stay this easy. Because eventually, we'll have to define this, and what if we're not on the same page? What if we break this by trying to put a name on it?"

He was quiet for a beat, his fingers still tracing absent patterns against her skin. Then he tipped her chin up again, forcing her to meet his gaze. "What if we don't?"

Her brows pulled together. "Don't what?"

"Don't break it. Don't overthink it. Don't let fear ruin something that just works." He exhaled, his thumb brushing along her jaw. "Kendrea, I don't need a label to know how I feel about you. And I don't need a label to know that I'm not going anywhere."

Her chest tightened, emotions crowding her throat. "And what if I need one?" she whispered.

Something flickered in his eyes, something that looked a lot like relief. "Then we'll figure it out. Together."

She searched his face, looking for hesitation, for uncertainty. But there was none.

Just Thomas. Just them. Just this quiet, effortless something that had wrapped around them so naturally, so completely, that she hadn't even realized how much she had come to need it.

Her fingers curled into the damp fabric of the towel around his shoulders. "Okay," she breathed.

A slow smile curved his lips. "Okay."

And then he kissed her—deep, sure, like a promise.

Kendrea didn't know what tomorrow would bring, but for now, she let herself melt into him, into the warmth of his arms, into the steady certainty of this moment.

For now, that was enough.

****

Thomas' birthday coincided with weigh-in day, month three. His sisters, Lori and Yasmin, were throwing a surprise party for him at Lori's restaurant. All Kendrea had to do was make sure he got there.

Thomas had lost forty-two pounds overall, and his body fat percentage had dropped to the teens.

"We have to celebrate this!" Amanda said.

"No can do," Kendrea replied. "I'm taking Thomas out tonight—it's his birthday."

"Oh." Amanda's eyes widened. "I didn't know that. Happy birthday, Thomas!"

"Thanks." Thomas stood behind Kendrea, subtly avoiding a hug from Amanda.

Kendrea chuckled.

"You didn't tell her it was your birthday?" she asked, glancing up at him.

Thomas shrugged. "Didn't come up."

Amanda pouted slightly but quickly masked it with a bright smile. "Well, I hope you have a great time tonight. You deserve it."

"Appreciate it," Thomas said, his tone polite but distant.

Amanda lingered for a moment before finally walking away, leaving Kendrea and Thomas alone.

Kendrea turned to face him fully, a mischievous glint in her eye. "So, what's up for today?"

"I come over to your store in the middle of the day, we put up the 'Closed' sign, and we make love in your office? Or you come over to my apartment, and we have lunch off each other's bodies?"

Kendrea laughed. "I'd do the second one, but I'm not into food play. That's weird. But since it's your birthday, and that's a fantasy of yours, I'll do it. Your fantasies have all been pleasurable so far."

Thomas laughed. "Happy birthday to me. I love having you as a girlfriend. Finally, someone I can be myself with."

Kendrea reached up to kiss him. "Later. I'm meeting a client this morning."

"It's not Dean, is it?" Thomas asked.

"Nope," Kendrea said, shaking her head. "Finished his project. His mother loved the décor so much she's recommending me to others."

"Okay," Thomas said.

"I like it when you're jealous," Kendrea chuckled.

"I hate feeling jealous," Thomas admitted, pulling her to him. "I feel possessive, and I don't want to be that guy. But with you…" He sighed, brushing a hand down her back. "I can't help it."

Kendrea smiled, pressing a kiss to his jaw. "A little jealousy is cute. Just don't go full caveman on me."

Thomas smirked. "No promises."

She pulled away with a teasing look. "Alright, birthday boy, go do whatever it is you do before lunch. I'll see you later."

He watched her walk away, shaking his head. She had him wrapped around her little finger, and the crazy thing was—he didn't even mind.

****

Hours later, Kendrea rolled out of bed and groaned. "We are going to be late. I am so happy I took a change of clothes this morning."

"What are we going to be late for?" Thomas asked sleepily.

"For your birthday dinner," Kendrea said, "come on."

"I already had a happy birthday," Thomas smirked. "We can stay here in bed and make it a happy birthday night and order takeout."

"Nope, we are going to dress up and go to Lori's restaurant to have dinner." Kendrea said, "If it were up to you, I'd never get out of bed."

"I have many years to make up for," Thomas said.

Kendrea chuckled. "I am not going anywhere, come on. I'll shower in the guest bathroom, and you shower in here. Don't take long. I am actually feeling a little more than hungry."

Thomas got up, stretching lazily before grinning at Kendrea. "Okay. We'll make a race of it."

"You say that like you don't already know I'll win," Kendrea smirked, grabbed her clothes, and headed for the guest bathroom.

"Only because I get distracted watching you," Thomas called after her.

They showered quickly, and by the time they were both dressed, Kendrea was practically pushing Thomas out the door.

When they arrived at Lori's restaurant, the place looked quiet from the outside. Thomas frowned. "Are you sure she's open tonight? The lights are kinda dim."

Kendrea bit her lip to keep from smiling. "Maybe she's doing a private dinner or something. Let's go in."

As soon as Thomas stepped inside, the lights flashed on, and a chorus of voices shouted—

"Surprise!"

Thomas stopped short, his eyes widening as he took in the scene. The restaurant was filled with his family and friends.

A big "Happy Birthday" banner hung from the ceiling, and the tables were decorated with balloons and streamers in his favorite colors.

Lori stepped forward, grinning. "Happy Birthday, little brother."

Thomas blinked, clearly caught off guard. "You guys did all this?"

"Of course!" Yasmin chimed in, walking up to hug him. "You thought we'd let your birthday pass without celebrating properly?"

Thomas let out a breath, shaking his head in disbelief before turning to Kendrea. "You knew about this?"

She grinned. "Maybe."

His expression softened as he stared at her, then at everyone gathered around. He looked like he didn't know what to say for a moment.

Lori clapped her hands. "Alright, enough staring! Let's eat!"

The party kicked into full swing, with laughter, food, and music filling the space. Thomas was pulled in every direction—his sisters fussed over him, and his friends all demanded his attention.

"Are you two together for real?" Griffin asked doubtfully. "I can never tell. You two are always tight."

"We are together," Thomas said. "We haven't said anything to anyone yet, but I do want to. I want to shout it from the rooftops."

Griffin grinned. "Congrats, man! My plan worked!"

"Keep your voice down," Thomas said. "Kendrea still doesn't know this was a plan. And we're not ready to be outed yet."

Griffin nodded. "My lips are sealed. But just so you know, you're looking at her like she's dessert."

Thomas chuckled.

His father knocked his fork against his glass to command attention.

"I have a speech," George Sterling said.

Silence descended on the room, and someone turned down the music.

"My eldest son is twenty-seven years old," George Sterling began, his deep voice carrying through the restaurant. "And I can honestly say I've never been prouder of the man he's become."

Thomas sat up straighter, his hands resting on the table. His father wasn't one for long speeches, so the fact that he was standing up to say something meant a lot.

"When Thomas sets his mind to something, he gives it his all," George continued. "And this past year, we've all seen that in more ways than one. He's taken his health seriously, his career is on track, and," his eyes flicked knowingly to Kendrea for the briefest moment before returning to Thomas, "he's surrounded himself with people who truly care about him."

Kendrea felt her face heat up, but she kept her expression neutral. Did his father know about them?

George raised his glass. "So, let's toast to Thomas. To another year of growth, happiness, and success. And to many more birthdays spent with family and friends who love him."

A chorus of "cheers" echoed as everyone raised their glasses. Thomas exhaled a small laugh, shaking his head as he clinked his glass with the people closest to him.

When the noise settled, Thomas leaned toward Kendrea. "You think he knows?"

Kendrea smirked. "Oh, he definitely knows."

Thomas groaned, rubbing his forehead. "So much for

keeping things quiet."

She squeezed his thigh under the table. "Could be worse."

"How?"

"Your dad could have announced our relationship in the speech."

Thomas laughed. "You're right. Small mercies."

Griffin nudged him. "Told you, man. You're not as lowkey as you think."

Lori reappeared with a huge chocolate cake topped with candles. "Alright, birthday boy, time to make a wish!"

Thomas looked around at his family and friends and finally at Kendrea, who was smiling at him in a way that made him feel like he could do anything.

"I don't need a wish," he said, locking eyes with her. "I've already got everything I want."

Cheers erupted again, and as Thomas blew out the candles, he had a feeling this was just the beginning of something even better.

Chapter Twenty

Thomas was going through a metamorphosis. His energy was up, his steps were lighter, and he looked different. It had been four months and two weeks since Amanda came into his life, and he was down a whopping fifty-five pounds. His face and belly were noticeably slimmer. Sometimes, he didn't even recognize himself in the mirror. Things were going right for him. It was amazing how much lighter he felt mentally and physically with the extra weight gone.

He was by no means near his ideal weight of 170 pounds, but the physical changes at his size were significant. He paused in front of the Deals and Wheels building. He could walk without wheezing. It was a good feeling.

"Thomas Sterling!" Nicole called from behind him. "Is that you?"

She removed her oversized sunglasses and blinked at him in confusion. "Oh my God, it is you! Where's the rest of you?"

Thomas glanced at her, then did a double take. Her face was swollen, she had a healing busted lip, and her eye had a gash with obvious stitches. She looked like a far cry from the well-put-together, gorgeous woman he had known.

"Nicole," he said with a frown. "You look banged up."

"Car accident," Nicole said. "It's not as bad as it looks. My airbag did a lot more damage than the impact. I wasn't even moving—something ran into me in the parking lot at my new business place."

"Poor you," Thomas said.

"Since I moved my store to Midtown, I've been having one bad thing after another happen to me, the pipes burst and wet up nearly all of my inventory, they have rats eating my shoes, and now this accident," Nicole said, hopping toward him. "I came to get some car parts my mechanic ordered. I can't get over how different you look."

Thomas smiled. "I lost some weight. I can see my toes again."

"My gosh," Nicole licked her swollen lips obscenely. "You even cut your hair. The lower cut suits you—it makes you look more debonair."

"Thank you," Thomas said with a nod.

He was about to walk away.

"Wait," Nicole said. "I've been meaning to tell you—sorry about the lawsuit. That never should have happened."

"You are forgiven," Thomas said.

"Are you seeing anyone?" Nicole asked.

"As a matter of fact, I am," Thomas said.

"Stupid question. Of course, you would be seeing someone," Nicole said. "You look great! Sometimes I think about what I gave up when I said those totally idiotic things to Abigail. I didn't mean any of it."

Thomas nodded. "That's nice to know."

"That's it?" Nicole asked. "I am willing to grovel to get back in your good graces."

Thomas arched a brow. "Grovel?"

Nicole nodded eagerly, stepping closer, her perfume still the same—vanilla and spice. "I was stupid, Thomas. You were the best boyfriend I ever had, and I let my ego ruin it."

He let out a short laugh, shaking his head. "You didn't let your ego ruin it, Nicole. You let your love of money and your need for status ruin it. You are nothing but a gold digger and I was your willing cash cow."

She flinched, but he didn't regret the words. Maybe months ago, he would've softened the truth to spare her feelings. But he wasn't that guy anymore.

Nicole sighed, looking down at her feet. "I deserved that." She looked back up, her gaze hopeful. "But people change. And I've changed."

"Maybe," Thomas said. "But I have, too."

Nicole searched his face, her swollen lips parting as if she had more to say, but Thomas wasn't interested in whatever plea she was about to make.

"I hope things start looking up for you," he said simply. "But I've moved on."

He didn't wait for her response. He turned and walked away, his steps lighter than ever.

His past didn't own him anymore.

And that felt better than any number on the scale ever could.

****

"Why am I not getting through to him?" Amanda fumed.

Stephanie was in the kitchen, deftly chopping vegetables

and listening to music. She popped out her headphones. "You said something, hon?"

"Yes!" Amanda snapped. "Thomas has become more withdrawn. It's as if the hotter he gets, the more he pushes me away. What gives?"

"He and Kendrea are banging," Stephanie said flatly. "I told you they were. And they look like two people who love doing it, too. The man has no time or energy for you—he's living on cloud nine."

"Liar!" Amanda screamed.

"Okay," Stephanie shrugged. "I told you the plan was a lost cause. We finish here in two weeks—what's next?"

"What's next is that I ramp it up with Thomas," Amanda said frantically.

"Please don't," Stephanie sighed. "I hate secondhand embarrassment. And I don't want to leave here under a cloud."

Amanda shot her a glare. "I don't care about your secondhand embarrassment. Thomas is mine. He just doesn't realize it yet."

Stephanie sighed, wiping her hands on a kitchen towel. "Amanda, listen to yourself. The man is clearly in love with Kendrea. He always has been. You can't force something that's not there."

Amanda slammed her hand on the counter. "I am not forcing anything! I'm just… reminding him of his options."

Stephanie arched a brow. "Options? Girl, please. You were never an option. He genuinely thought of you as his health coach—nothing more."

Amanda's jaw tightened. "That's not true. When he looks at me, there is something there."

"He looks at you the way someone looks at an old receipt—briefly and with zero interest."

Amanda's eyes flashed with anger. "You're wrong."

Stephanie sighed again, picking up her knife. "I really hope so, for your sake. Because if you push too hard, you're gonna humiliate yourself. And I, for one, am not sticking around to watch that."

Amanda clenched her fists, ignoring the sting of Stephanie's words. She wasn't giving up. Not yet.

****

The next morning, they were in the gym. Amanda admired Thomas as he effortlessly did his pull-ups on the bar. At this point, he didn't really need her anymore. He was familiar with his routines—he was even developing his own based on fitness videos he watched.

She was superfluous.

He had successfully changed his old habits and was looking amazing in five and a half months. His body was strong, and sculpted in a way that made it clear he had put in the work. Broad shoulders, defined abs, powerful arms—he was the picture of dedication and discipline.

And yet, despite all his progress, despite how much time they had spent together, she felt him slipping further and further away.

Amanda's lips pressed into a thin line as she watched him drop from the pull-up bar. His breathing was steady but barely winded. He grabbed a towel, wiping the sweat from his brow, before reaching for his water bottle. He hadn't even noticed her staring.

"Looking good, Thomas," she said, forcing a bright smile.

He glanced at her, gave a small nod, and took a sip of water. "Thanks."

That was it. No teasing. No lingering glance. No invitation

for more conversation.

She folded her arms. "So, what's the plan for today? Do you want to go through some resistance training or focus on core work?"

Thomas shook his head. "I actually have my own routine planned out for today. You did say it was carte blanche day. I am preparing my own routines so that I have a template when you leave."

Amanda felt her stomach twist. It was happening—she was being phased out.

"Oh." She forced a chuckle. "I see someone's feeling confident."

He shrugged. "I've learned a lot. Thanks to you, of course."

His words sounded like a closing chapter, like gratitude before moving on. Amanda couldn't let that happen.

"Well," she said, stepping closer and tilting her head. "I guess I'll have to find another way to make myself useful to you."

Thomas gave her a polite but distant smile. "You've already done plenty, Amanda. I appreciate it."

She hated that. The appreciation. It wasn't what she wanted. She wanted desire, longing, and interest. But he was already glancing at the clock, already mentally checking out of this conversation.

And Amanda knew exactly where his mind had wandered. Kendrea.

It was always Kendrea.

Her fingers curled into fists at her sides as she watched him move to the hamstring curl machine, completely unaware of the storm brewing inside her.

No. She wasn't going to be forgotten that easily. If Thomas thought he could just brush her aside, he had another thing coming.

"Where's Kendrea this morning?" she asked. "Usually, she doesn't leave you alone."

Thomas smiled. "She's sleeping in. She was working on a project that kept her up last night."

"Aww," Amanda said without sympathy.

"You don't have enough weight on the machine," she said abruptly, changing the subject. "Let's see if you can work your hamstrings with an additional one hundred and thirty pounds." She straddled his leg and sat on him.

Thomas looked at her with incredulity. "Amanda… what the hell are you doing?"

Amanda gave him a sweet, innocent smile, feigning ignorance. "What? You wanted more weight, didn't you? Consider me an extra challenge."

Thomas let out a sharp breath, his jaw tightening. "Get off."

"Come on, Thomas," she purred, leaning in slightly. "I'm just helping you push your limits."

His hands immediately went to her waist, gripping firmly as he lifted her off and set her aside like she weighed nothing. Amanda barely had time to react before he was towering over her.

"That was completely inappropriate," he said, his voice dangerously low.

Amanda huffed, brushing imaginary dust off her leggings. "Oh, please. Don't act like I'm some random woman off the street. We've spent months together. I've seen you at your lowest and helped you become what you are now." She crossed her arms. "A little gratitude wouldn't kill you."

Thomas let out a humorless laugh, shaking his head. "Gratitude? Amanda, I am grateful. But that doesn't mean you get to cross boundaries like that."

"Boundaries?" Amanda scoffed. "Funny, I don't see you

setting those with her."

His expression darkened. "If you're talking about Kendrea, then yeah, you're damn right I don't. Because what's between us is real. And she actually respects me."

Amanda clenched her fists, heat rising to her face. "You think she respects you? She's just waiting for you to get bored, Thomas. She sees you as a safety net, not a man."

Something in Thomas's eyes shifted—cold, sharp. "You don't know anything about Kendrea and me."

Amanda took a step closer, her voice softening. "I know you, Thomas. And I know that deep down, you like my attention. You like feeling wanted. Kendrea's too comfortable, too familiar. But me?" She trailed a finger down his arm. "I see the man you're becoming. I see your potential."

He caught her wrist, his grip firm but not harsh. "You need to stop."

Amanda searched his face, waiting for any flicker of hesitation, any sign that he wasn't as immune as he pretended to be. But there was nothing.

He dropped her hand like it burned him.

"I love Kendrea," he said simply. "And no amount of whatever this is will change that."

Amanda stared at him, chest rising and falling, the truth cutting through her like a blade.

He wasn't hers to manipulate anymore. But she had one more ace up her sleeve. Sex. What man could resist a naked woman?

She pulled up her top, revealing her breasts.

Thomas paused for an infinitesimal second, staring in frozen shock.

"Amanda, please, don't do this." His voice was low and husky.

"Do what?" Amanda asked, taking advantage of his stunned inaction. She reached up and kissed him.

"Oh my God!" Kendrea's voice rang out from the doorway.

Thomas jolted back like he'd been burned, shoving Amanda away with more force than necessary. His eyes were wide with panic as he turned toward the doorway.

Kendrea stood frozen, her expression unreadable, but her grip on the doorframe was white-knuckled.

"Kendrea," Thomas started, his voice thick with urgency. "This isn't what it looks like—"

Amanda let out a breathless laugh, wiping the corner of her mouth. "Isn't it?" she taunted.

Thomas whipped around to glare at her. "Shut up, Amanda."

Kendrea finally moved, her arms folding across her chest, her face eerily calm. "So what is it, then?" she asked, her tone deceptively light.

Thomas shook his head, his heart hammering. "She—she did this on purpose. I didn't—"

"I kissed him," Amanda cut in, her voice smug. "And, well…" she gestured to her exposed chest. "He didn't exactly look uninterested."

Kendrea's jaw tensed. "Wow," she murmured, then exhaled a slow breath. "I need a second—nope, make that a couple of hours."

"Kendrea, please," Thomas took a step forward.

But she was already turning away, walking briskly out of the gym.

Thomas shoved his fingers into his hair, breathing hard. "You just made the biggest mistake of your life, Amanda."

Amanda smiled, shrugging her top back on. "We'll see about that. It's your word against mine. I'll tell anyone who will listen that you assaulted me. But I won't say a word if you just give us a chance, Thomas. I hate that it's come to this."

"Once a bully, always a bully," Thomas sighed. "I thought you had changed. Why me? Why now?"

"Because I like you and want to be with you," Amanda said. "My contract is coming to an end, and you haven't shown the least bit of interest in me. I had to do something to force a reaction."

Thomas stared at her, disgust twisting in his gut. "So you thought blackmail was the way to go?" He shook his head. "You don't like me, Amanda. You like control. And you hate that you don't have any over me."

Amanda's lips pressed into a thin line. "I'm offering you a way out, Thomas. You can fight me on this and risk a scandal, or you can just—"

"Just what?" he cut in, his voice like steel. "Throw away everything I love, betray Kendrea, lie to myself just to keep you quiet?"

Amanda lifted her chin. "You'd be surprised how many men have made worse choices for less."

Thomas exhaled, rubbing a hand down his face. Then he laughed—low and humorless. "You're right about one thing," he said. "I do like who I've become. And that man doesn't bow to threats."

Amanda's smug expression faltered.

"I won't give you a damn thing," Thomas said coldly. "And if you so much as think about spreading lies, I'll make sure everyone knows exactly what you did here today."

Amanda's face twisted in fury. "You can't prove anything."

"I can prove it. There's video footage of the gym," Thomas said, sighing. "I actually thought you were different."

"There is?" Amanda's eyes widened. "Please, forgive me," she pleaded. "I don't know what came over me."

"You don't see me as a human being," Thomas said, disappointment heavy in his voice. "I'm either a meal ticket or a gold mine. You thought I would be an easy target."

Tears ran unchecked down Amanda's face.

"If I didn't have Kendrea, I'd be so disappointed in the female species right now," Thomas inhaled raggedly. "You better hope she sees this morning for what it was. Because if I lose the one woman who loves me for me, Amanda—I will destroy you. And I will take pleasure in doing it."

Amanda gasped.

"By the way, you're fired," Thomas said. "You've taught me well—I can handle my weight loss from here on out. I'll have my secretary courier your check for this month, minus the bonus I was going to give you. And I want you gone from my guest house by the end of the day."

Chapter Twenty-One

Kendrea drove off before he could catch up to her. Only then did he realize that she had been dressed to go out.

Thomas ran his fingers through his hair, exhaling sharply. What on earth was running through her mind? Was she furious? Would this put a crack in their relationship?

His hands trembled with uncertainty.

He headed for the shower, letting the hot water pound against his tense muscles before dressing and glancing at himself in the mirror. Some days, he hardly recognized the man staring back at him. He had worked hard for this transformation, but at what cost? If Kendrea didn't trust him after what she saw, then what was the point of any of it?

Grabbing his keys, Thomas hurried out, dialing her number.

"Kendrea, please pick up," he muttered, listening to the call ring out. Twice, it went straight to voicemail.

Frustration simmered under his skin. He knew her well enough to know she wouldn't just sit and stew—she needed space. But too much distance could turn a misunderstanding into something worse.

Where was she heading? The office? A meeting with a client?

His stomach twisted, but he forced himself to think rationally. He might as well eat something while he kept trying her phone.

When he entered the kitchen, he found Stephanie standing by the counter, staring into space. She wasn't wearing her usual headphones, but the moment she saw him, her face came alive with regret.

"Oh, Thomas… I need to apologize for what Amanda did. I knew she was up to something but never thought she'd take it this far."

He shook his head. "You don't have anything to apologize for. I'll be sorry to lose you most of all… I know you're a package deal with her."

Stephanie gave a small nod. "I was planning to return to the States anyway. I only came here to help her get her business started. But after this… well, that's pretty much over."

Thomas shifted awkwardly. "I really enjoyed your meals." He wasn't sure what else to say. One thing was certain—he wouldn't be recommending Amanda to anyone.

Stephanie offered a sad smile. "Thanks. I liked cooking for you guys. And for what it's worth, I think Amanda really did like you. Just… in a twisted, possessive way."

Thomas scoffed. "That's not liking someone. That's obsession."

She sighed. "Yeah, I know. But she never takes rejection well. And Kendrea walking in when she did? That's going to make things worse."

Thomas ran a hand over his face. "I need to find Kendrea before Amanda spins this into something it wasn't."

Stephanie nodded. "She left pretty fast, huh?"

He exhaled sharply. "Didn't even give me a chance to explain."

Stephanie hesitated, then asked, "If you were her, would you have stayed?"

Thomas opened his mouth, then shut it. She had a point. If he had walked in on Kendrea with another man like that… His blood boiled at the thought.

"I still have to fix it," he muttered.

Stephanie reached for the teapot and poured him a cup of green tea. "You will. You guys will work it out."

He took the tea and nodded. "Yeah."

As he sipped, his mind raced through the places Kendrea might have gone.

Her best friend's house? Her office? Somewhere to clear her head?

He had to think like her—to find her before this misunderstanding turned into something irreparable.

Then it hit him.

She would go somewhere that made her feel safe. Somewhere familiar.

Thomas grabbed his keys. "Thanks for the tea, Steph. But I think I know where she is."

And he was going to prove to Kendrea that no misunderstanding, and no manipulative woman was going to come between them.

****

She was sitting in the living room of the apartment above

the store—his old place. They had taken to going there for lunch together since they worked in such close proximity, and sometimes, they had a little more than lunch.

"Oh, there you are," Thomas said after he let himself in. "I checked your store first. Your new assistant said you didn't feel well."

Kendrea nodded. "I don't. I had a meeting with Richard Tinsdale and canceled it."

"About this morning…" Thomas leaned on the door and pushed his hands into his pockets. "I fired Amanda."

Kendrea nodded. "I expected you would."

"Are you going to say, 'I told you so'?" Thomas raised an eyebrow.

"No." Kendrea inhaled shakily. "That's the reason you asked me to live with you in the first place—to safeguard you against this very thing happening."

"Actually, that's not the reason I asked you to live with me," Thomas said softly. "It was all Griffin's plan at first. He thought hiring Amanda would be a good way for us to get closer—you'd get jealous of her, draw closer to me, and I'd have the added bonus of weight loss."

"I see." Kendrea chuckled.

"She laughs." Thomas walked closer. "Is this a good sign?"

"It is." Kendrea nodded.

"You do know she threw herself at me out of nowhere, don't you?"

Kendrea shrugged. "It wasn't out of nowhere."

Thomas frowned. "What do you mean?"

Kendrea exhaled and met his gaze. "Amanda's been making moves on you for weeks, Thomas. Maybe not as blatantly as today, but she's been testing the waters. I saw it. Stephanie saw it. You just…" She shook her head. "You didn't want to see it."

He ran a hand down his face. "Damn."

"You were focused on your fitness goals, on your progress. And I get that. But Amanda was always a predator, waiting for the right moment."

Thomas sat beside her on the couch. "I hate that she put you in this position. That you had to witness that."

Kendrea studied him for a long moment before she spoke. "Do you regret hiring her?"

"Of course," he said immediately. "If I had known she'd pull something like that—"

She waved a hand. "Not just because of today. I mean everything. Do you regret the journey?"

Thomas hesitated. The past five and a half months had changed him completely—physically and mentally. But at what cost?

"I don't regret getting healthier," he admitted. "I don't regret feeling stronger. But if it made you doubt me, if it made you feel like you were losing me…" He took her hand, lacing their fingers together. "Then I regret that part."

Kendrea bit her lip as if weighing his words. Then she squeezed his hand. "I never doubted you, Thomas."

He exhaled in relief.

"I doubted her."

A small smile tugged at his lips. "Smart woman."

Kendrea tilted her head. "You said Griffin planned this whole thing. What was your plan?"

"My plan?" He grinned. "I planned to love you regardless and hope you'd love me too."

She stared at him, her expression softening. "I love you so much."

"So, what do you say we make things official?" Thomas asked. "Lock down your man before I lose a couple more pounds and drive all the women crazy in these parts?"

"I'd say yes." Kendrea smiled.

He reached down to kiss her, his lips brushing against hers with a tenderness that made her heart ache in the best way. Kendrea melted into him, her fingers threading through his hair as she deepened the kiss.

Thomas pulled her closer, his arms wrapping around her like he never wanted to let go. And maybe he didn't.

When they finally broke apart, he rested his forehead against hers. "You have no idea how long I've wanted to hear you say yes."

Kendrea smiled, running a hand over his jaw. "Then you should've asked sooner."

He chuckled. "I was waiting for the right moment."

"And this is the right moment?"

He kissed her again, slower this time, savoring every second. "It's the perfect moment."

The End

Excerpt Tried and True (Book 4 Ridgeview Series)

Anise sat in the monthly Spice and Stone Division meeting, vaguely listening as her nephew, Leo Greystone, the head of the division, droned on and on about the launch party for their newest wine, Bay Rock. It was their first vegan wine and Leo's brainchild—because he was dating a strict vegan who refused to touch their other wines.

Leo was so excited about the finished product he could burst. Anise sat on the opposite side of the conference table as he ran through the virtues of the wine and its taste. So far, however, he had yet to address the actual plans for the launch—the very reason she was there and why he had urged her to attend.

Her title at Greystone Wines was Wine Exploration Director, an honorary position that allowed her to dabble in wine development without the burden of actual responsibility. She wasn't trained in winemaking, nor did she pretend to be, but she had an instinct for flavors and a deep appreciation for the art of it all. Most of the time, she simply enjoyed showing up for tastings, making a few dramatic pronouncements about what worked and what didn't, and then retreating to her life outside the winery—managing her beauty supply shop.

Today, however, Leo had been adamant that she attend this meeting.

"Your opinion matters, Anise," he had said, flashing that Greystone charm that usually got him whatever he wanted.

She shifted in her chair and crossed her legs, letting her gaze drift to the glass of Bay Rock set in front of her. Deep ruby red, its color was inviting, almost sensual. She lifted it, swirling the wine with an expert flick of her wrist before bringing it to her nose. The aroma was pleasant—bright fruit with a hint of earthiness. She took a sip, letting it linger on her tongue.

"Not bad. Surprisingly smooth."

Leo paused mid-sentence, watching her expectantly. The room had gone silent. Anise set the glass down deliberately, pressing her lips together in thought. She could practically hear Leo's heartbeat from across the table.

"It's good," she said finally. "I really can't tell the difference between this and our other wines. And I love the name Bay Rock."

Leo smiled. "That's a relief. We intend to name all the vegan lines with 'Rock' at the end, kind of like a series. However, we'll only move ahead when we see how well this does on the market."

"Can we move on to the launch party aspect of the meeting?" Anise asked impatiently. "I have a thing somewhere else."

"As usual, Anise, I know your skin starts to itch if our meetings run even a smidge over fifteen minutes," Leo said with a smirk.

The table chuckled. They knew her by now. If you wanted her attention, you had to give her bullet points—no frills.

"It's a side effect of my ADHD," she said. "You all know that. Now, get to it."

"Okay, moving on," Leo said quickly. "I was thinking of a romance theme for the launch."

"Perfect," Milly, one of the marketing execs, said. "When I first tasted Bay Rock, romance came to mind. Not to mention it's red, and Valentine's Day is six weeks away."

"We could do a Valentine's launch," Leo nodded. "That was at the back of my mind—make it a grand celebration of love. We could have DJ Duke headline for us."

"That alone will sell the tickets," Milly said. "But six weeks is short notice to book the hottest singer on the airwaves right now. That song of his, It's Always You, is all I hear on the radio. Getting him to perform live would be impossible."

Leo shook his head. "I would agree with you, but we have a secret weapon." He peered down the table at Anise.

Anise shifted in her chair. She didn't know what Leo was getting at, but she didn't like how he was grinning at her suggestively—like he knew something. Her relationship with Duke Jones was a secret. As far as the world knew, she was single and unattached. And she liked it that way. Her life these days was peaceful and free of press intrusion.

"What are you talking about?" she asked, clearing her throat.

"This." Leo pointed to a magazine. "The headline reads, Are They Together or Not? The writer says, 'This is the third event where I've spotted DJ Duke and Anise Crystal hanging out together. Are they an item? Watch this space.'"

Anise rolled her eyes. "Rubbish. I hang out with people and they write about it all the time."

"The picture tells a story, though," Leo mused. "Duke is looking at you with unconcealed adoration."

"Let me see that," Anise grunted.

Leo passed the magazine down the table. It moved slowly—everyone wanted a look.

When she finally got it, she sighed. The picture was taken a week ago at their mutual friend's birthday party—right when Duke had given her an ultimatum.

"I'm tired of us hiding, Anise. Something's got to give. I'm tired of being on the outside of your life, looking in. I want to shout it from the mountaintops—I don't care who knows."

But she cared. She didn't want to let the public in. Or her family. Or anybody else, for that matter. She wanted to keep this relationship under lock and key, away from prying eyes and outside opinions. Because, for the first time in her life, she was hopelessly and stupendously in love.

"Anise," Leo prompted. "Since you are allegedly close to DJ Duke, in whatever capacity, can you ask him to perform for us on Valentine's Day at our Bay Rock launch?"

Anise looked up at Leo. "Of course I'll ask him."

"So, are you two dating?" Milly asked eagerly.

Anise leveled Milly with a look, her expression unreadable. "What does that have to do with the launch party?" she asked coolly, taking another sip of her wine.

Milly grinned but backed off. "Just curious."

Leo, however, wasn't letting it go that easily. "You didn't deny it," he sing-songed, tapping his fingers on the table.

Anise sighed, setting the glass down with a little more force than necessary. "I said I'd ask him, didn't I?"

That was all they were going to get out of her. She wasn't about to confirm or deny anything—not in a room full of people, not when she and Duke were still trying to figure things out. He was ready for the world to know. She wasn't. He wanted marriage and children. She was a mother of three, a grandmother of two and she felt as if she had done all of that already.

And that was the problem. The only fly in their ointment.

Leo, satisfied for now, clapped his hands together. "Alright, moving on. We'll finalize the venue and guest list this week. Milly, start working on a promo strategy. If Duke agrees, we'll build a campaign around that."

The meeting wrapped up quickly after that, much to Anise's relief. As everyone shuffled out, Leo caught up with her at the door.

"You know," he said, lowering his voice, "if you really love him, you can't keep him in the shadows forever."

Anise stiffened. "I don't…"

Leo held up a hand. "Not my business. But just think about it." He patted her shoulder before walking away, leaving her standing there, her stomach twisting.

Discover Exclusive Offers and Be the First to Know!

If you haven't already, don't miss out on the opportunity to join my New Release Newsletter! Sign up today and become part of an exclusive community where you'll be among the first to hear about my latest book releases and take advantage of special prices.

Why join my mailing list?

Be the First: Get a head start and be the first to know when I release a new book.

Exclusive Discounts: Unlock special prices available only to subscribers. Enjoy limited time offers and save big on your favorite books.

Quick and Easy: Signing up takes less than 30 seconds.

To join, visit https://www.brenalbar.com/newsletter or scan the QR code below.

Thank you for your support, and happy reading!

Ridgeview Series

The Ridgeview series follows five couples on the Jamaican north coast in the luxurious community of Ridgeview. It explores their everyday struggles with careers, children, and family drama. Each book touches on love, marriage, and trust as the characters face challenges that test their relationships.

Ride or Die (Book 1)
Play For Keeps (Book 2)
Through Thick and Thin (Book 3)
Tried and True (Book 4)
Stay With You (Book 5)

Spice and Stone Series

Join three extraordinary girls—Cinnamon, Cayenne, and Sage—as they navigate the intricate flavors of life, love, and romance in the captivating Spice and Stone series.

Cinnamon (Book 1)
Cayenne (Book 2)
Sage (Book3)

The Crimson Hill Series

Where family drama, romance, and a touch of sci-fi blend seamlessly in the enchanting backdrop of a small town in Jamaica. Prepare to embark on an unforgettable journey as secrets unravel, passions ignite, and destinies intertwine.

No Goodbye (Book 1)
No Misunderstanding (Book 2)
No Ordinary Love (Book 3)
No Fairy Tale (Book 4)
No Letting Go (Book 5)
No Strings Attached (Book 6)
No More Mrs. Nice Girl (Book 7)
No Place Like You (Book 8)
Knight and Day (Book 8.5)
No Expectations (Book 9)
Ice and Fyre (Book 9.5)
No Surrender (Book 10)
No Time for Love (Book 11)
No Promises (Book 12)
Winter's Eve (Book 13)

The Wiley Brothers

Step into the world of the Wiley Brothers, where tragedy weaves an unbreakable bond and love becomes their guiding light. In this captivating series, follow the journey of six remarkable boys as they navigate the tumultuous path of growing up without parents, discovering love, and finding their place in a challenging world.

Between Brothers (Book 0)- How it all began…
For Pete's Sake (Book 1)- Preston's story.
Crossing Jordan (Book 2)-Jordan's story.
Fire and Walter (Book 3)- Walter's story.
The Perfect Guy (Book 4)-Guy's Story.
The Patience of a Saint (Book 5)- Saint's Story.
A Case of Love (Book 6)- Case's Story.

The Pryce Sisters

Follow the remarkable journey of the Pryce triplets as they navigate the complexities of growing up, discovering romance, and embracing the exhilarating challenges of the new adult years.

Baby For A Pryce- Book 1
Right Pryce Wrong Time – Book 2
Yours, For A Pryce- Book 3

The Jacksons

Prepare to be enthralled by the captivating saga of the Jackson family. In this gripping series, secrets unravel, paternity questions loom, and love blooms in the most unexpected corners.

Ace- Book 1
Deuce- Book 2
Trey- Book 3
Quade- Book 4

The Scarlett Series

Their patriarch died and unexpectedly left each of them a fortune. Watch as the Scarlett family navigate their way through the ups and downs of sudden wealth, family secrets, and the complicated dynamics of their relationships.

Scarlett Baby (Book 1)
Scarlett Sinner (Book 2)
Scarlett Secret (Book 3)
Scarlett Love (Book 4)
Scarlett Promise (Book 5)
Scarlett Bride (Book 6)
Scarlett Heart (Book 7)

Magnolia Sisters

They were the rejects. The worst of the lot, they grew up in a girl's home together and formed sisterly bonds. Each book in the series tells the story of a different girl and the unique struggles and triumphs she faces along the way. With themes of friendship, forgiveness, and the power of love, the "Magnolia Sisters" series is a heartwarming and inspiring read that you won't want to put down.

Dear Mystery Guy- Book 1
Bad Girl Blues- Book 2
Her Mistaken Dream- Book 3
Just Like Yesterday – Book 4

New Song Series

A group of friends started out as a church band, see how each of them navigate their personal and professional lives while staying true to their faith and facing challenges along the way. With themes of forgiveness, redemption, and second chances, the New Song Series is a captivating read for anyone who enjoys heartwarming stories of love and faith.

Going Solo- Book 1
Duet on Fire- Book 2
Tangled Chords- Book 3
Broken Harmony- Book 4
A Past Refrain- Book 5
Perfect Melody- Book 6

The Bancrofts

The Bancroft family delves into the inner workings of academia and the high-stakes world of university politics. The family wrestles with the pressures of maintaining their family's legacy, they must confront their own demons and navigate the complex relationships that bind them together. From unexpected love affairs and betrayals to scandals and secrets that threaten to tear them apart, this is a series that will keep you captivated until the very end.

Homely Girl- Book 0
Saving Face- Book 1
Tattered Tiara- Book 2
Private Dancer- Book 3
Goodbye Lonely- Book 4
Practice Run- Book 5
Sense of Rumor- Book 6
A Younger Man- Book 7
Just To See Her- Book 8

Three Rivers Series

Three Rivers Series, a captivating tale of love, redemption, and second chances set in a picturesque community in St. Ann's Bay, Jamaica.

Private Sins- Book 1
Loving Mr. Wright- Book 2
Unholy Matrimony- Book 3
If It Ain't Broke- Book 4

The Resetter Series

The Resetter Series takes a look at a rare kind of person, a person who can travel back in time, but they only have one chance to get things right if they go back! With themes of second chances, changing the past and the power of love, the resetters series is a captivating time travel romance that many readers have described as a page turner.

Never Too Late- Book 1
Never Say Never- Book 2
Now or Never- Book 3
Almost Never- Book 4

On the Rebound Series

Experience the gripping and emotionally charged On the Rebound series, where love, betrayal, and redemption collide in a whirlwind of passion and secrets. Brace yourself for a journey filled with drama, cheating scandals, DNA questions, and ultimately, the power of second chances and finding love again.

On the Rebound- Book 1
On the Rebound Book 2

Standalone Books

Full Circle- After graduating from university, Diana wanted to return to Jamaica to find her siblings. What she didn't foresee was that she would meet Robert Cassidy and that both their pasts would be intertwined, and that disturbing questions would pop up about their parentage just when they were getting close.

After the End- Torn between two lovers. Colleen married her high school sweetheart, Isaiah, hoping that they would live happily ever after, but life intruded, and Isaiah disappeared at sea. She found work with the rich and handsome Enrique Lopez as a housekeeper and realized that she couldn't keep him at arm's length.

Love Triangle: Three Sides to the Story- George, the husband. Marie, the wife, and Karen-the mistress. They all get to tell their side of the story.

New Beginnings- Inner-city girl Geneva was offered an opportunity of a lifetime when she learned that her 'real' father was a wealthy man. Her decision to live up-town meant she had to leave Froggie, her 'ghetto don,' behind. She also found herself battling with her stepmother and battling her emotions for Justin, a suave up-towner.

The Preacher and the Prostitute- Prostitution and the clergy don't mix. Tell that to ex-prostitute Maribel, who finds herself in love with the Pastor at her church. Can an ex-prostitute and a pastor have a future together?

Historical Fiction

You won't want to miss out on these two captivating reads!

"The Pull of Freedom" tells the story of a slave family and their desperate struggle for freedom in Jamaica's colonial era. Follow the journey of these brave individuals as they fight for their right to be free, facing danger, heartbreak, and unimaginable obstacles along the way.

"The Empty Hammock" takes readers on a journey through time, as a modern woman finds herself transported back to the Taino era of Jamaica's history. Experience the wonder and mystery of this ancient culture through her eyes, as she learns about their traditions, beliefs, and way of life. With richly drawn characters and a beautifully realized setting, "The Empty Hammock" is a must-read for anyone who loves historical fiction that transports them to another time and place.

Short Story Collections

Di Taxi Ride and Other Stories- Funny stories about Jamaican life to make you laugh.